Sunshine & Silk Boxers

WELCOME TO KISSING SPRINGS

JOI JACKSON

The Welcome to Kissing Springs Series

Read all 27 books across 3 seasons by 9 authors.

Santa Season:

Welcome to Kissing Springs

Sunshine Season:

Welcome to Kissing Springs: Sunshine Season

Bourbon Season:

Welcome to Kissing Springs: Bourbon Season

To my husband
Thank you for supporting my crazy idea to write novels. I appreciate you each and every day.
Love you forever,
Joi

CHAPTER 1

Winston

"Oooo...how do you turn that up? That's my song!"

Winston Locke took his eyes off the road to watch his closest friend, Gia Mitchell, as she attempted to crank up the volume on his custom car audio. "It's voice controlled...Jarvis, turn the volume up by thirty percent."

The volume rose, filling the car with Erykah Badu's *Ode to Hip-Hop.*

Peering at her, Winston decided he'd let the marriage talk go for now. Since he was in town to help her get her lingerie boutique off the ground, he'd have plenty of time to convince her that marriage was a good thing, and they would make a great couple.

Gia rapped along, grinning and gesturing as though she was on stage with a mic in her hand. During a break in the lyrics, she tapped him. "Remember this? From the Brown Sugar Soundtrack? We saw that together and you rolled your eyes the whole time. I saw that movie three times while it was in the theaters."

He sighed. They were both in college at Kentucky State University back then. And, as he recalled, taking Gia to that movie had cost him a girlfriend at the time. She couldn't fathom that he and Gia were only friends, even though he'd tried to assure her they were more like brother and sister than lovers.

"I rolled my eyes because there is no way anybody would leave Nicole Ari Parker for Sanaa Lathan. Just not happening. It was unrealistic," Winston said.

"They were best friends! Destined to be together...I don't see how you don't get that." She continued to sing along. "And they shared a love of hip-hop. Very important relationship foundation if you ask me."

He rolled his eyes again. "Yeah, well, maybe that's why my ex left. She felt more of a hip-hop connection with my friend."

She picked up his phone from the holder and after a few finger motions, the music stopped. "Sarah was a piece of work who didn't deserve you. Understand that. I knew she was trouble the first time I met her."

"You didn't say anything." It wasn't an accusation; he knew why she didn't, he wouldn't have listened.

"No, I didn't," she sighed. "I wasn't gonna make you choose between her and me," she said finally.

Before he could comment that he'd always chosen her, she cranked up another Erykah Badu classic.

He let her have her concert while he drove. This felt almost like their college days when they didn't have many responsibilities and they were hanging out together all the time. During their college years, he spent holidays in Kissing Springs with Gia's family since he had nowhere else to go.

"So, what's it like being back in town after all these years?"

They were headed to Two-Fourteen, an upscale restaurant in downtown Kissing Springs, for lunch with Gia's mentor and her son.

Gia turned the music down. "It's weird, on one hand, it's familiar, lots of the same people I knew growing up, but Kissing Springs has changed so much these last few years. Not such a sleepy small town anymore but not exactly Manhattan either. And my family has changed. My mother still does her passive-aggressive thing with me but, Win, my parents are world travelers now. They're going on a fourteen-day European cruise in a couple of weeks. When I was growing up, the furthest we went was Florida and that was only because we had relatives there."

"I thought the town looked bigger than I remembered. We had some good times here. And again, I don't know what I would have done without your parents letting me stay with you when school was out."

"You know they consider you family now, right? I think my mother would trade me for you in a heartbeat if she could. She does better with sons."

"Your mother loves you, she's just not sure what to do with you. You're more outspoken than she was," Winston assured her.

"Let her tell it, I'm more everything than she was. She asked me why I wanted to do lingerie instead of ready to wear. She thinks I should be the next Vera Wang or Monique Lhullier and do designer wedding gowns. I've no interest in being a bride, so why do wedding gowns?"

Winston's heart sank. He'd hoped that she'd softened her stance over the years, but she was still adamantly against marriage. "So, you just planning to stay single and get cats or what?"

"Ugh, I'm allergic to cats, so no on that. I don't know, I just don't see myself getting married and giving up my life to be someone's wife. Plus, I'm going back to New York once I make this store a success. I'm living life on my own terms, and I love it. No plans to change." She pointed at the turn in for the restaurant's parking lot. "I may get a dog at some point. We'll see."

Gia hummed the Erykah Badu song again as Winston pulled into a parking spot near the entrance. "Question for you...why didn't you tell me your mentor was international supermodel Skye?" he asked as he turned off the ignition.

"I didn't do it intentionally; sometimes I forget how big a deal she was because to me she's just my friend and she's retired from modeling. She's like the non-judgmental older sister I always wanted," Gia said, crossing her arms. "I've never met her son though. She doesn't talk about him much."

Winston nodded. "Well, I guess we'll meet him in a few. Is he a model too?"

"No idea. All I know is that he's in his twenties."

* * *

Winston glanced at his table mates. Was it just him who felt the tension in their booth? As soon as the man across from him appeared, like a dark cloud, the mood at the table went south.

The booth was roomy enough with four people, two men and two women, but things were awkward now.

To his left, Gia was doing her best to avoid looking at the man. Gia's friend and mentor Skye was next to Gia and Andreas was sitting next to his mother and across from Winston.

Table tension aside, he still couldn't believe he was sitting at a table with the actual Skye. She was a former lingerie supermodel and the object of many of his teenaged fantasies. Skye the supermodel was holding court, talking about her recent trip to Milan. The woman, now in her mid-fifties, if he had to guess, was still striking. Her wavy platinum hair was cut in a chic pixie and her eyes were a piercing shade of green. She was tall with a graceful posture that carried through her body. She wore an air of confidence that made her even more beautiful.

He hadn't expected her to be so...normal.

Sipping his beer, he watched her. Skye frequently patted her son's arm like any other doting mother. Although, if he was being honest, she struck him as a bit of a helicopter mom even though her son was clearly grown and on his own. Skye, he knew from the media, bounced between coasts, choosing to spend the winter months in LA when she wasn't in New York, but Andreas mentioned he'd been living in Nashville before he moved to Kissing Springs.

Winston sensed all was not well with mother and son.

Andreas seemed tense, his jaw tight, like he might snap at any moment.

He felt a slight tremor. Gia was sitting close enough that he could feel her leg bouncing every few seconds. Dead giveaway that she was nervous.

He reached under the table, placing a firm hand on her knee. The bouncing stopped.

Her eyes met his and she gave him a brief, grateful smile. Gia had transformed into a beautiful woman after college. She was cute and awkward back then, but she'd been his ride-or-die best friend and now she was this stunning, powerhouse lingerie designer. She had dyed her long, coily, jet-black hair a warm cinnamon color that matched her skin.

Winston felt eyes boring into him. Directly across from him, Andreas drummed his fingers on the table. Apparently, he'd caught the look he and Gia shared. His green eyes, which Winston could see came from his mother, were narrowed and Winston knew he was being sized up by the younger man.

As he tried to gauge where the animosity from Andreas was coming from, a thought occurred to him. Maybe Andreas thought Winston was after his mother. He was sure his starstruck gawking was obvious to the whole table.

A sliver of envy wormed its way through Winston. Andreas was everything he wasn't: young, attractive, and looked like he'd never lacked for anything. He'd seen women doing double takes as he strode through the restaurant toward their table. And Gia, he noted, wasn't immune to his looks. She had barely glanced Winston's way since the younger man arrived.

As they waited for their food, Winston looked around Two-Fourteen, taking in the elegant decor and luxurious atmosphere of the upscale restaurant. The walls were adorned with tasteful art pieces; the lighting was dim but warm, and the tables were covered in crisp white linens with polished silverware and crystal glasses. The hushed murmur of conversation and soft piano music provided a soothing background to the dining experience.

Although he ate at nice restaurants regularly now, this was the kind of place he'd never dreamed he'd frequent when he was growing up in Frankfort. Back then, a trip to McDonald's and sharing a kid's meal with the other foster kids he lived with was a rare treat.

Winston shifted in his seat, feeling like he was missing something. The way Gia and Andreas kept throwing furtive glances across the table had him wondering how they knew each other. He couldn't quite put his finger on it, but something was definitely going on between them.

Their food arrived and everyone dug in. Winston cut into his steak, his mouth watering.

During a lull in the conversation, Winston cleared his throat. "So, Andreas, what brings you to town?"

Andreas glanced at Gia before turning to him. "I'm here for a job. Entertainment marketing," he said.

"Ah, sounds interesting," Winston replied, hoping the man would elaborate, but Andreas offered no further details.

There was an awkward pause then Gia nodded. "Yeah, it definitely is." There was something in her voice, a slight edge that he picked up on but couldn't understand. He glanced at her, his brow furrowed, but she was staring straight ahead.

Skye dabbed at her mouth with her napkin. "Well, this is such a coincidence! Gia, you can help Andreas get situated in town and Andreas might be able to help with some promotional events. I don't really get the whole small-town thing but this could be a big opportunity for you both."

Winston watched as Gia and Andreas silently nodded in agreement to Skye, but neither said anything. The air between them seemed to grow more tense with every passing moment.

Finally, Gia spoke up. "Skye, how long are you going to be in the US?"

Skye had a very busy schedule for the next few months which she dove into describing with great detail, but Winston couldn't focus. He kept stealing glances at Gia and Andreas, both of whom were pretending to listen to Skye while attacking their food.

Winston slathered butter on his baked potato. He had known Gia for years, and he had never seen her act so nervous around anyone before. Something had changed.

* * *

Later, after they bid goodbye to Skye and Andreas, Winston opened Gia's door for her then settled into the driver's seat. He left the car off and turned to her.

"Gia, what's going on between you and Andreas?" Winston asked, getting straight to the point.

She didn't respond immediately, and he waited, drumming his fingers on the steering wheel.

"Why do you assume something is going on?"

"Really? I know we haven't seen much of each other since I moved to Chicago, but come on, give me some credit." He studied her face. "I saw the way you two were looking at each other." Winston persisted. "And when he wasn't peeking at you, he was staring me down, almost like I was infringing on his territory."

Gia sighed, looking down at her lap. "Fine, I'll tell you. We had a one-night stand in Nashville. I never thought I'd see him again."

He waited for her to say she was kidding. "Hold up, you're serious?"

She nodded, not meeting his gaze.

"Gotcha." Yep, that would explain the dirty looks from the man. Winston leaned back in his seat. "And now he's here, working at the male stripper place, Derby Nights?"

Gia nodded again. "Yeah. And it's clear Skye has no idea what he's doing."

Winston shook his head. "I mean, he's grown, what's she going to do, storm in there and tell them to fire her baby boy?"

Winston chanced a glance at Gia. "How old is he anyway?"

"He's twenty-nine." Gia rubbed her forehead, groaning. "Don't judge me."

Winston's fists tightened at hearing Gia's confession. He wanted to yell at her for sleeping with Andreas, but he bit his tongue. She had a right to do whatever she wanted. But that didn't mean it didn't hurt him. His heart sank into the pit of his stomach.

He rubbed his forehead. "I've never known you to be reckless...what made you sleep with a stripper of all people? God knows where he's been. You didn't pay him, did you?"

Her head snapped around. "Of course not! He's not a prostitute." She crossed her arms. "You think I'm that desperate for male attention?"

Now he'd pissed her off.

He softened his tone. "No, I'm just trying to understand. This isn't like you."

Gia huffed. "Men do this all the time! He's a good-looking man with a great body who seemed to be into me, so I invited him to my room for the night. That was supposed to be it. Now he apparently lives here in my town where everybody knows everything about everyone else."

"You don't think he followed you here, do you?" Winston asked.

"I don't think so. I mean, I never told him where I was from. I guess he could have looked me up online and found out, but I would think he would see that my info was all New York based and look for me there." She studied her hands. "He looked as shocked to see me as I was him."

"I don't know. Something seems off." He started the car. "You should keep an eye on him."

She nodded absently, playing with the gold chain around her neck; he could tell something was on her mind. He wanted to pull her against him and tell her everything would be fine.

"It's awkward, I feel like I'm kinda in the middle of this big secret he's keeping from Skye, but it's not my place to tell her, is it? But I'd want to know if my son was taking his clothes off for money."

He thought she should steer clear of both parties, but she wouldn't want to hear that. Instead, he squeezed her hand, wanting to make her feel better somehow. "I think he'll tell her when he's ready. You shouldn't be the one to break that news to her."

Relief washed over Gia's face. "Yeah, I think you're right," her eyes softened as she smiled at him, placing a hand on his arm. "I'm so glad I have you here."

Winston's chest tightened as he felt the warmth of her skin. He wanted to confess his feelings to her, but he knew it was too soon. He had to keep his emotions in check, at least for now.

CHAPTER 2

Gia

A few days later, Gia donned her best *I mean business* dress, a sleeveless poppy red midi with a mandarin collar and red heels then set out for the government buildings in the center of town.

She breezed into the executive area, stopping at the front desk. "Hi, could you tell the mayor that Gia Mitchell would like to speak with her?" Gia tapped her foot nervously and tried to keep the annoyance out of her voice. Working with the lower-level government employees had gotten her nowhere and now she was starting at the top.

Gia stood, glaring at the only person available, a dark-haired young woman, who looked about her niece Jordyn's age, who Gia assumed was a summer intern. The woman looked up from her laptop screen, her eyes wide. "I'm so sorry, Ms. Mitchell, but Mayor Boyd is out of the office today."

Sighing, Gia softened her tone. She shouldn't take her frustrations out on the messenger. "Do you know when she'll be back?"

The young woman shook her head quickly. "She's actually on vacation for the rest of the week. Is there anything I can help you with?"

Gia bit her lip and thought for a moment before finally deciding that there wasn't anything else she could do without speaking directly to the mayor. "No, I suppose not. Could you tell her I stopped by and that I would like to meet with her as soon as possible when she returns?"

The young woman nodded, typing rapidly on her laptop. "Of course, ma'am, is that Gia with a J or a G?"

"It's a G, thanks."

The woman gave her a sympathetic smile. Gia thanked her again then she strode out of the office into the bright Kentucky sun, swearing at the heat and humidity. It wasn't even ten yet. Digging into her purse, she pulled out a pair of sunglasses and stood, annoyed, in the center of town.

Now what?

She needed to talk to someone about her permit requirements and until she did that, construction on her store was halted. Time was indeed money, and she couldn't afford to lose out on a whole week.

Gia trudged down the sidewalk, hot and annoyed, her feet aching from the red peep toe heels she'd been foolish enough to wear today. The shoes were cute but not meant for walking more than a few steps at a time.

A cold drink would help. She turned and headed toward French Kiss Coffee, one of the many new businesses that had popped up in town since she'd moved away. Slipping inside, she was thankful for the cool air that hit her as soon as the door closed behind her.

Gia ordered an iced coffee and moved to the side to wait for her drink.

As she stood there, Gia couldn't help but overhear the conversation at the table next to her. Two older women were discussing the new businesses that had been popping up around town.

"It's ridiculous, that's what. Kissing Springs as a tech hub. All they're doing is replacing honest, God-fearing workers trying to feed their families with robots." The woman sitting closest to Gia scowled at her friend. "You hear that new robotics company is taking over the space where the old automotive plant was? My husband got laid off when that plant closed and hasn't worked since."

"I know. Maybe you need to send him over to Derby Nights," the other woman cackled. "I hear they're still looking for dancers."

Gia tried to ignore the women's conversation, but her ears perked up at the mention of Derby Nights. She wondered if Dre had started work there.

The first woman snorted. "I'd rather starve than see my husband stripping for a bunch of horny housewives, thank you very much."

The second woman tsked. "Speak for yourself. I heard those dancers make a pretty penny. And they're damn fine to look at, too. They're over at the theater rehearsing now, we should go check it out."

Scowling, the first woman waved a dismissive hand. "You're too old for that foolishness. Finish your coffee so we can get to Bingo before all the good seats are taken."

Gia rolled her eyes, stifling a smile. The women looked to be in their sixties, around her mother's age, and she could see her mother turning her nose up at the thought of gambling. And visiting a strip club. And probably, Dre. Not that she would ever consider bringing him home to meet her family. That was for serious contenders for her heart, which a one-night stand most certainly was not.

As she waited for her drink, Gia's mind wandered to their night in Nashville. She had never been the type of woman to have a fling, but there was something about Dre that had drawn her in. Maybe it was the way he looked at her, or the way he moved on stage. Whatever it was, she couldn't deny that she wanted him that night.

They'd had a good time and parted ways the next morning.

He hadn't asked for her number or even her last name and she'd been fine with that. Usually, men like him had a steady rotation of willing women to choose from, and given his profession and good looks, he probably had more than his share.

After that night, she'd wondered about him. Gia had always been curious about people's back stories. She was curious to know how he'd gotten into exotic dancing and now that she'd learned he was Skye's son, she wanted to know how he ended up so far from his mother. Skye had mentioned her son in passing, saying that he'd left home as soon as he was able, but Gia never heard Skye say that he was in town or that she was going to visit him. She called him Andreas.Gia would never have made the connection.

The barista yelled her name, holding her drink.

With her heart pounding, Gia made a decision. On a whim, she grabbed her iced coffee and strode out of the coffee shop, headed in the direction of Derby Nights. She was fairly certain Dre would be there rehearsing and she needed answers from him.

Gia walked with purpose, her heels clicking on the pavement as she made her way towards the theater. The closer she got, the more her nerves kicked in. She considered Winston's question. Surely Dre hadn't moved here because of her? That was ridiculous; they hadn't exchanged any personal information. How would he even know how to find her? She guessed if he was savvy enough on social media, anyone could be located, but she was careful not to share more personal detail than necessary.

Her mentor, Skye, clearly didn't know they knew each other, and she was the only person who might have connected the two. She squared her shoulders. She should just ask already.

As she grabbed the brass handle of the door and pushed, her heart thumped in her ribcage. The scent of sweat and the noise of blaring music flooded her senses. Gia's eyes took a moment to adjust to the dim lighting, but as they did, she saw Dre, shirtless and dripping with sweat, on stage with three other men, working through a hip-hop routine.

Gia stood motionless, watching intently as the four men

moved their bodies in perfect unison, their muscles flexing with each movement. Dre was in the front row, his lean frame moving fluidly as he executed each step with precision. His brown skin glistened in the dim light, his muscles taut and defined. Gia couldn't help but feel a stirring in her lower belly as she watched him move.

The other three men were just as impressive, their bodies chiseled and toned as they moved together as one. They wore athletic shorts and white sneakers squeaked on the wooden stage. The dance was meant to be suggestive, to hint at what the men were capable of doing behind closed doors.

Her breath caught in her throat at the sight of him. He was even more beautiful than she remembered, his muscles rippling as he moved to the rhythm of the music. Gia felt a flush rise to her cheeks as she watched him, her body responding to the sight of him in ways she couldn't control.

Maybe this wasn't such a great idea.

He'd been hers for one night, letting her call the shots and catering to her whims. It might be nice to... maybe...

She blinked.

Nope. She wasn't going there again. One night only.

One of the dancers called for a five-minute break and the men hustled from the stage.

As two of the dancers passed, the shorter of the two paused, giving her the eye. "What's up, *Mami?*"

The other man shoved him forward. "Off limits. That's Jameson's little sister."

The man stepped back like he'd been burned. "Sorry," he muttered.

Gia frowned, wondering what her older brother had said to warn the men off. She knew the dancers used Jameson's gym for their workouts. Another reason she'd hightailed it out of town after college. Not that she'd had many boys interested, but her overprotective brother had made dating nearly impossible.

She watched, unable to drag her gaze away as Dre picked up a large water bottle and took a long drink. Those green eyes that she'd dreamed about often since their night together met hers.

Gia froze for a split second, her mind going blank. She tried to appear unaffected as he approached her.

A smile tugged at the corners of Dre's mouth and Gia had trouble remembering why she was so annoyed minutes ago. "Well, I can't say I'm surprised you tracked me down," he drawled, his voice deep and smooth. "What are you doing here?"

Gia's heart skipped a beat at the sound of his voice. "Imagine my surprise at seeing you in my hometown, Andreas," she said, trying to sound casual.

Dre tilted his head to the side, his eyes scanning her from head to toe. "Yeah, seemed like the joke was on both of us. And call me Dre."

"So, Dre, what are you doing in Kissing Springs?" Gia decided to get right to the point.

He shrugged, not meeting her eyes. "A couple of the guys from Nashville told me they were hiring and convinced me to audition. The pay is much better, and the cost of living is lower, so here I am."

His words were too rehearsed, too neat. Gia's skepticism must have shown on her face.

Dre's expression turned serious. "Look, I know it probably looks like I followed you here," he paused, running a hand over the back of his neck. "I'll admit to Googling you after we met, but I promise I'm not a stalker." He raised his head, his eyes searching hers intently.

She could tell he'd let his guard down, at least partially, and she felt the sincerity.

Gia's heart raced. "Good to know," she said crisply. "What about your mother? She doesn't know about any of this?" She motioned to the stage.

Dre ran his hand through his hair and sighed. "No, she doesn't. I plan to tell her eventually, but for now, the less she knows, the better. It's...complicated."

Gia nodded, understanding why Dre might want to keep this a secret for now. She knew his mother was going to be furious when she found out about his career choice. Image was everything to Skye.

"Our show premiers in one week and we are far from ready!" A voice bellowed through a loudspeaker. "Back on stage, from the top!"

Dre looked toward the stage. "I gotta go," he sighed reluctantly, "but I want to talk to you about something. In private."

Gia's heart skipped a beat at Dre's words. "Ok, this sounds serious," she said slowly. "Anything I need to be worried about?"

She watched him debate with himself. "Are you ok with coming to my place after I'm done here?"

Before she could respond, he added quickly, "I'm not trying to push up on you or anything, just," he glanced around, "I feel like there are eyes and ears all over this place."

That sounded ominous. And he hadn't answered her question. "Um, sure, I can do that. What's your address?" Taking her phone from her purse, she handed it to him.

"Last call! I need asses and elbows on the stage now!" The loudspeaker startled Gia.

Dre typed quickly. "Thanks," he said, passing the phone back to her. "I'll be done by five, then I'm heading straight home."

Gia nodded, dropping the phone into her purse. As he turned to make his way back to the stage, Gia couldn't help but feel a flutter of excitement in her stomach. What did he want to talk about in private? And why did they need to be so secretive? And most important, why was he really in Kissing Springs?

She had more questions than answers, but she'd figure things out later when they met up. Part of her was looking forward to being alone with him again, even though she knew this wasn't a social visit.

CHAPTER 3

Dre

Once rehearsal ended for the day, Dre stopped by J&J Fitness, the gym all the Derby Nights dancers used to keep their bodies in performance ready condition. He did some stretches, refilled his empty water bottle then eased himself into the sauna. He'd pushed his muscles to their limits today, but the routines were looking good.

Making sure the towel around his hips was secure, Dre leaned back, breathing in the warm, moist air and letting his mind wander. He'd invited Gia over on impulse and his apartment wasn't visitor ready at all. After their night in Nashville, he never expected to see her again. Now she was coming to his place. Anticipation coursed through his veins. Despite having only seen her three times, Dre was deeply attracted to her.

He, however, wasn't going to pursue anything with her. She'd pretty much made it clear that she wasn't interested in him beyond that one night and he didn't need the complications. She was too close to his mother.

With that decision made, Dre languished in the sauna until the timer sounded and then hit the shower.

As he was repacking his gym bag and preparing to head home, he saw Jameson Mitchell, the gym owner, striding through the locker room with one of the men who did maintenance. Jameson nodded a greeting at Dre as they passed, but he was clearly explaining something to the man.

Dre had been meaning to talk to Jameson. He checked his watch. He had a little time before he needed to get home. He slung his gym bag over his shoulder and made his way to Jameson's office at the back of the gym. The door was closed and Dre flopped onto a bench to wait.

He watched Jameson and the maintenance man approach. When they looked up and saw him sitting there, the man nodded and left Jameson.

The older man walked up, holding his hand out for Dre to shake. "It's Dre, right? You're one of the new guys from Nashville?"

Surprised, Dre nodded, shaking his hand quickly. "You got it. Do you have a second?" Dre had heard his co-dancers comment that Gia was Jameson's sister and now that he was up close, he could see some resemblance. Their skin coloring and facial features were very similar.

"Sure, sure, come in and have a seat." Jameson opened the office door and motioned to the chairs in front of his desk. "How's the town treating you so far? Not Nashville, I know, but this is a nice place to live."

"Good so far. Your gym is one of the best I've been to," Dre said, looking around the office.

"Thanks, I've always loved fitness, and this is my way of helping people stay active. But I'm sure you didn't come in to hear me ramble. What's up?" Jameson sat then tented his fingers.

Straight to the point, just like Gia.

"Well, I heard you have some youth programs that you run here at your gym, and I was wondering if you were doing any dance instruction or lessons for them? I'm thinking about creating a dance studio for families who can't afford lessons."

His brow furrowed; Jameson sat back in his chair. "You teach dance?"

Dre shrugged. "I did a bit of teaching before I started dancing in Nashville. I'm classically trained, Alvin Ailey, actually, but this pays much better."

To his credit, Jameson didn't act surprised, as people tended to do when they found out he was a professional dancer. Since he'd started dancing for male revues, Dre was used to people judging and underestimating him.

Nodding, Jameson picked up a small notepad. "I took my wife to an Alvin Ailey show in Charlotte. I didn't think I'd enjoy it but man...I was amazed." He tapped his pen on the notebook. "Anyway...I like the idea and I'm always looking for something that will hold the kids' attention. Have you put together any sort of schedule?"

He hadn't thought that far ahead. "No, but I was thinking a hip-hop class for starters a couple times a week?"

"I like the idea," Jameson said hesitantly. "The only thing is that some of the parents may think you're teaching the kids how to, um," he winced, "dance for tips."

Dre hadn't thought of that either. "I guess I could see where they'd be concerned. Maybe we can call it more of a dance fitness type class."

Jameson held up a finger. "Here's an idea...you could do a demonstration at the schools. My wife works at the high school but she can connect you with staff at the other schools. Show the kids what the classes will be like."

"Oh yeah, I've done that before with The Ailey School. I still have contacts there. I'll ask about getting some of them to come as well."

"Man," Jameson grinned, "if you could pull that off, my wife Noemie would love that! Let's do it. Let me know what you're thinking in terms of classes and timeframes, and we can schedule it around the group fitness classes. Also, if you're interested, there are some buildings around here coming up for lease that might work as a dance studio. You probably haven't met her yet, but my sister Gia got a great deal on her building."

Dre kept his expression neutral, realizing Gia hadn't mentioned to her brother that she knew him. He glanced at his watch. He needed to hurry home and straighten up.

"I'll put together my ideas and send them to you," he said, taking a business card from the stack on Jameson's desk. Dre held it up. "I've got your email."

"Yeah, do that," he cocked his head. "I'm sure you're meeting a lot of women at the shows, but do you have a special lady friend yet? Maybe you can bring her to dinner with me and Noemie? We can go over to Two-Fourteen."

A lady friend. He had to stifle a grin. What would Jameson say if his sister appeared on Dre's arm as his date?

Jameson seemed like a good guy and under different circumstances, Dre would have enjoyed a dinner outing with the couple, but another awkward meal at the fanciest restaurant in town was the last thing he needed.

"I don't really have time to date these days," Dre admitted. "I'm still trying to settle in." The move from Nashville to Kissing Springs had been more jarring than he expected. He missed the energy and bustle of the city. He felt more isolated than he thought he would.

"Oh yeah, you got kids?" Jameson asked.

Dre shook his head. "Nah, no kids."

"Man, enjoy being single and carefree," Jameson said. "Plenty of single women in town and I'm sure they're all over you."

Dre shrugged, unwilling to share details of his non-existent love life with Gia's brother. Anything he said could make its way back to her.

While women at his shows used to excite him, the thought held little appeal now. They liked the fantasy of his stage persona, not the real man behind it. He couldn't explain it, but he sensed Gia was different. The cynic in him assumed great sex was clouding his judgment but he chose to ignore that train of thought.

Just as Dre stood up to leave, Gia's friend from the lunch

stuck his head in Jameson's office. Dre frowned. What was the man's name? Wilson? William?

"My man, Winston! Come in, have you met Dre?" Jameson motioned for Winston to enter the office.

How was he supposed to answer that question without opening a huge den of snakes? Before he could respond, a cell phone on Jameson's desk rang, and he held it up, "Give me a minute."

Dre and Winston stepped out of the office to give him privacy.

Greeting Winston with a head nod, Dre asked, "What's up, Winston?"

When Winston didn't respond, Dre eyed the older man. Winston needed a trim, the unfashionable fade haircut greying at the temples. He wore baggy sweats and an old t-shirt that had seen better days. Winston's once muscular frame had gone soft around the middle. To Dre, the man looked like he could be Gia's dad.

Once Jameson shut the door, Winston glared at Dre like he might attack. "Andreas. What are you doing here?"

"It's Dre."

"Whatever. What are you doing here?" Winston repeated.

Where was all the hostility coming from? He raised an eyebrow. "What most people do at a gym...keeping my body in shape," Dre said, gesturing to his toned physique before throwing a pointed look at Winston's gut. "Something you might want to consider."

Winston's face twisted in a scowl. "Talk to me when you get a real job, you know, one where you actually keep your clothes on."

Dre chuckled. "A real job? I'll bet I make more in one Friday night than you do in a week."

Winston sneered. "Yeah, I'm sure you're doing more than stripping to earn it. Come on, Dre. That's not a real job. Real men work for a living." He spat the last words, as if Dre's line of work was beneath him.

Dre folded his arms. "Oh really? So, sitting in front of a

computer all day makes you more of a man than me?"

Winston's eyes narrowed. "I'm making people's lives better. You're just a pretty face with no substance."

Dre's expression turned cold. "Is that what you think? You really have no idea who I am, do you?"

Winston shrugged. "Why should I care about Gia's random one night stand who doesn't have the guts to tell his mommy he's screwing women for pay."

Dre started to tell the man exactly what he thought of him when he noticed the gym had grown quiet. The crowd was light at that hour, but all of the members were watching the heated exchange, enthralled.

Swearing under his breath, Dre turned toward the door. This was not the first impression he wanted to make in Kissing Springs. "I'd love to stand here and trade insults with you, but I have better things to do with my time."

"Yeah, like what? Go back to your little strip club and shake your ass for a bunch of horny women?"

Dre made sure Winston met his gaze. "No, actually, Gia's waiting for me."

For a fleeting moment, Dre enjoyed the shocked look on the man's face, but then his eyes narrowed. "We'll see about that."

"I guess we will." Dre strode out of the gym.

* * *

After rushing home, Dre hurriedly changed into a pair of cargo shorts and a tank top. Then he quickly set about tidying up his apartment, shoving clothes into the closet, and throwing dishes into the dishwasher. He glanced at his watch. He'd told her he'd be home by five and that time was almost up. Gia struck him as the punctual type, and he expected she'd be knocking on his door at any moment.

Nervous energy had him adjusting and readjusting everything. There were still moving boxes that needed to be unpacked but he'd gotten all the major stuff done. He hadn't made time to organize his kitchen yet; the cabinets were bare, save plates, silverware, and cups. The box of pots and pans had been shoved in a corner which meant he didn't have anything to cook with. What if she was hungry?

He could order takeout, but he'd do that after she arrived. He didn't want to give her the impression this was a date and scare her off.

He grabbed a beer from the fridge and settled onto his couch, wondering what he should say when Gia arrived. Should he just come out and tell her what he wanted to talk about? Or should he take it slow and ease into it?

He popped up from the couch, pacing.

Why couldn't he sit still and wait? Inaction wasn't his nature; he knew as he strode to the kitchen to pull a bag of kale chips from the small pantry. He had something to talk to her about and, he finally admitted, he wanted to see her.

Contrary to what he'd said about not being totally surprised she'd found him, when he looked up during rehearsal and she was standing there in that sexy red dress and heels, he assumed his fatigue was causing him to hallucinate. Dre's day started at five in the morning with a three-mile run then straight to the theater for rehearsals.

He had just finished cleaning up and making sure everything was in order when the doorbell rang. Taking a deep breath, Dre ran a hand through his still damp hair and opened the door.

Gia stood on the other side, her eyes taking in his place before she met his gaze. "Hey," she said softly.

Dre allowed himself to gawk at her for a few seconds. Gia was striking yet approachable, with smooth mocha skin and a dazzling smile that lit up her whole face. She'd changed from the dress she wore earlier into a more casual pair of walking shorts, and a frilly yellow top. Her wild curly hair was pulled into a high ponytail. While she was more athletic than voluptuous, her walking shorts hugged her curves and shapely legs that went on for miles.

Dre knew exactly how good those legs felt wrapped around his waist.

He'd assured her that he wasn't going to try anything while she was here. He'd need to remember that, regardless of how sexy he found her.

"Hey," Dre said, stepping aside so she could come in. "Welcome to my humble abode."

Gia smiled as she walked in. He watched her take in the space then her focus was on him. "Your place looks comfy and lived in already! I figured you'd still have tons of boxes piled up. You just moved here, right?"

"It's been about a month," he said. "Have a seat on the couch. Can I get you anything? Water, soda, anything?"

Gia shook her head. "I'm good," she said, taking a seat on one end of the sofa. "So, what did you want to talk about?"

Dre hesitated.

Gia rushed on, running her fingers over a gold chain around her neck. "Sorry, I tend to jump right in. I don't do small talk very well." She sat back, resting her arm on the sofa. "How are you liking Kissing Springs so far?"

Chuckling, Dre took a sip of his beer. "You're fine. I'm still getting used to the small-town vibe, but yeah," he stroked his beard, trying to figure out where to start. "So, I told you I Googled you. I wasn't trying to stalk you or anything, I was just curious. The lingerie idea was fascinating," he explained. "But then I saw this article on 3D printing in fashion where you were quoted as saying you used a 3D printer to create patterns."

She seemed pleased that he knew what she was talking about as she nodded with enthusiasm. "Yes! That was in one of the entrepreneurship magazines I've blogged for, but what does that have to do with anything?"

"Are you planning to use 3D printers for your merchandise in the new store?" He enjoyed seeing her geeky side surface and knew she could probably talk tech for hours.

Dre smiled, transfixed by her energy, and watched as she

talked animatedly about 3D printing and the applications it had in fashion. He was so engrossed he didn't realize he had leaned forward until his eyes met Gia's. Her gaze was intense and focused on him and electricity shot through him.

His heart skipped a beat as an urgent desire to kiss her again hit him. He'd anticipated kissing her that night they met when she'd invited him to her room, but now that he knew exactly how it felt when their lips touched, the thought of it sent a thrill straight to his groin.

"I managed to get a 3D printer that will design lingerie and then print the fabric. It's amazing! Custom pieces to fit in a fraction of the time a mass production facility would take. And since the town is always full of brides and bachelorettes, I'm projecting I'll have plenty of customers."

Dre was impressed. "That sounds like a great idea," he said. He paused for a moment, thinking before he asked his next question. "You know there's a robotics company coming to town, right?" He didn't wait for her answer. "Well, I don't know if you've heard but there's a growing number of residents who don't want the plant or any other tech firm. They think the companies won't or don't need to hire local help so they're organizing."

He looked at her. "I think you may end up in their crosshairs."

Gia's smile dissolved. "I heard there was a robotics company coming but that has nothing to do with me."

Dre could tell by the way Gia's back stiffened that he had struck a nerve. He knew he had to tread carefully.

"I just thought you should be aware," he said, taking a sip of his beer. "I don't want to see your business suffer because of some disgruntled locals."

Gia took a deep breath and let it out slowly. "Thanks for the heads up," she said eventually.

Dre watched as she wrapped her arms around herself, as if suddenly cold. He knew he had upset her and wished he could help.

"Sorry," he said quietly. "I didn't mean to be the bearer of bad news, but I figured you would want to be prepared."

Gia shook her head, her eyes distant. "It's not your fault," she said, her hand on the chain again. "I just...I've put so much into this business, you know? It's my dream, and I don't want to see it fail because of something that's out of my control."

"You've got a great concept, and everything might be fine, I just wanted to let you know what I've heard from the guys and their families. These guys I work with, they gossip like high school teens."

Gia managed a small smile. "Thanks for looking out for me," she said, leaning back into the couch.

There was a charged silence between them as they sat next to each other, their bodies almost touching. Dre could feel the warmth of her skin and her familiar floral scent evoked memories of them together in her hotel room. He knew he was in danger of losing control if he didn't do something to distract himself.

"So, are we addressing the huge hippo in the room?" Gia asked, her voice lowered.

He raised a brow. "It's an elephant, I thought?"

"Hippos are more aggressive and much more dangerous. So bigger issue, bigger threat."

He shot her a look, not sure where she was going with the question. Right now, his hippo in the room was baring his tusks and urging Dre to tell her he wanted to carry her to his bed, feel her underneath him again, screaming his name. He ran a hand over his beard. Probably not the time for that conversation. Not when she likely still thought he'd found her online and followed her here. He could tell she wasn't totally sold on his explanation.

He took the coward's way out. Dre held out his hand, palm up. "Ladies first."

Gia played with the piping on the sofa cushion. "There are probably a million reasons why I should get up and leave right now, forget Nashville, and act like we barely know each other when I see you around. You didn't move here for some other woman, did you? Or have some chick wondering why you're not answering your phone right now?"

He let out a soft snort. "With rehearsals and trying to learn all the Derby Nights routines plus get situated in town, I barely have time to eat, so no."

Gia nodded. "From what I saw, you all looked good...but same here. So, I'm figuring that since we're both extremely busy, and this attraction doesn't seem to be going anywhere, maybe we help each other out?"

Dre couldn't believe his ears. Was Gia really suggesting what he thought she was suggesting? He couldn't deny that he was definitely attracted to her, she wasn't far from his thoughts since the night they spent together.

"What do you mean?" he asked, trying to keep his voice steady.

She looked at him straight in the eye, her gaze unwavering. "I mean, we both have needs, and we're both consenting adults. Think about it. No strings attached, no commitment, just the two of us enjoying each other whenever the mood hits."

Dre felt a thrill shoot straight through him at Gia's suggestion. He knew he was feeling her, but he didn't expect her to reciprocate his feelings. He knew he should be careful, not wanting to ruin their newfound friendship, but he couldn't resist the temptation.

Dre peered at her. He did have another hippo to discuss. "What about the dude you were with at the restaurant? Something tells me he's going to have a problem with our arrangement."

"Winston? No, we're just friends," she said, dismissing the question, "He's fresh out of a breakup."

Crossing his arms, Dre didn't believe that. "You sure? He seemed awfully protective of you."

"No, we've never crossed that line. I've known him since college; it's sweet that he looks out for me but we're more like brother and sister."

He leaned forward, his voice low. "Ok, good to know, cause I don't want to ever be viewed as your brother."

She scooted closer to him. "No worries there. Now that the hippo has been put down, shall we start the agreement now?"

"No time like the present," he said, his hand reaching out to touch her face.

Dre's heart was pounding in his chest as he leaned forward and kissed Gia. Her lips were soft and inviting, and he could feel himself slipping deeper and deeper into the moment. His hands moved to her waist. Breaking the kiss, he stood and took her hand, pulling her to him before bending to continue exploring her mouth.

Dre felt Gia's soft moan as he ran an urgent hand under her shirt, resting on the small of her back before he tugged her closer, flush with his erection.

His hand slid down to palm the swell of her hips.

She was fumbling with his belt buckle when a loud voice rang through the apartment from the bedroom.

"Flash News Alert. Gia Mitchell. Morris Mitchell Designs announces IPO."

Gia's hands dropped to her sides, and she stepped away from him.

"Device off," he said quickly. *Shit.* Dre closed his eyes, running a trembling hand down his face. He knew this looked bad.

"What kind of stalker shit is this? You've got news alerts for my name?" Her voice was shaky, and she winced slightly, grabbing her right side. "Why did you move here?"

"I...ah," Dre tried to come up with a plausible explanation but stopped. he peered at her in alarm. Gia had gone slightly green. "Are you ok?"

"Why didn't you just ask me whatever you wanted to know?" She stepped away from him, snatched her purse from the couch then dropped it suddenly.

He watched, shocked, as the color leeched from her face.

"Where's your bathroom?" Her breathing was heavy like she'd just run up a flight of steep stairs.

"Are you going to be sick?" he asked, pointing toward the hallway. He was kicking himself for asking such a stupid question as she bolted toward the bathroom.

He debated on following. Did she need help? Would she even want his help now that she viewed him as a stalker?

He heard the retching and his heart thudded.

Dre took off toward the sound as she vomited again.

When he stepped into the bathroom, she was sitting on the side of his bathtub, poised to vomit into the toilet again. She retched, but nothing came out.

Grabbing a clean hand towel from the linen closet, Dre dampened it with cool water and handed it to her.

Gia reached for it, groaning, and grabbed her stomach instead. "Oh God...my side...hurts."

She was nearly doubled over in pain, her forehead drenched in sweat as Dre placed the towel against her. She was too warm. A random thought hit him. "Have you had your appendix removed yet?"

Wearily, Gia shook her head and Dre hustled out of the bathroom to grab his phone to look up the nearest hospital.

He grabbed Gia's purse and strode back to the bathroom. She was rinsing out her mouth when he entered. He held her purse out. "I think your appendix is either infected or it's burst so I'm taking you to the hospital."

She shook her head. "No, it's maybe... something I ate..." Gia bent again, grabbing her side. "No hospital," she grunted. "I'll go to the doctor tomorrow."

Dre led her out of the bathroom. "How about you humor me and we get you checked out so we know for sure."

Gia stopped. "No, I don't want you to take me anywhere. I'm going to call my brother."

She reached for her purse and collapsed against him.

CHAPTER 4

Winston

Winston's eyes followed Dre as he exited the gym. Was he bluffing about Gia waiting for him? He debated calling her, but he wasn't sure what he'd do if she confirmed his fear. His mind raced with thoughts of how to get Gia to see that Dre wasn't right for her.

Consumed with thoughts of both his own inadequacies and his desire for Gia, Winston knew he needed to make a change, to better himself physically and mentally if he had any chance with her. He couldn't help but feel envious of Dre's physique, his youth, all of it.

Jameson opened the door to his office and glanced around. "Dre left?"

Winston nodded and Jameson motioned for him to enter and take a seat. "Sounds like you and Dre had words just now? What was all that about?"

Running a hand over his neck, Winston sat down. He still couldn't believe he'd let Dre get under his skin. "Nothing. I lost my cool and got into a little pissing contest with him. It's done."

Winston felt the heat of Jameson's stare. "Did I hear my sister's name? What's Gia got to do with it?"

He sighed, hoping Jameson would let the matter drop. "They know each other. Dre is Gia's mentor's son."

"Really? Dre is Skye's son? I didn't know Skye had any kids. When Gia told us Skye was her mentor and investing in her shop, we were shocked. My sister is big time," Jameson said proudly.

"Yeah, well, Skye has no idea Dre is a stripper," Winston said. "So, if you get to meet her, don't say anything."

Jameson grunted. "For a small town, this place sure keeps its share of secrets."

"Unfortunately, I have one I'd like you to keep as well." Winston rested his elbow on his knee and took a deep breath. Time to swallow his pride and ask for help. "Jameson, can we talk for a minute?" he asked hesitantly.

"Sure thing, Win. What's on your mind?" Jameson asked as he leaned back in his chair, studying Winston

"I need to get in shape," Winston admitted, his gaze landing to his flabby stomach. "And I think I need your help to win Gia over."

"Son of a bitch...I owe my wife a couples massage," he muttered, staring at Winston.

"What?"

"Noemie called it. She said you have feelings for Gia and I insisted that you both were just friends." Jameson raised an eyebrow. "You do realize my sister is the most headstrong, stubborn person I know and she's not going to appreciate any meddling in her life?"

Winston nodded, "Yes, I know that. But I've let myself go since my broken engagement and I need to do something to change my life, and to change her perception of me. I can't keep feeling like I'm not good enough for her."

Jameson studied Winston for a moment before finally nodding. "All right, I can help you. Let's start by putting together a workout schedule and some meal plans. We'll take it one step at a time and see where it goes."

* * *

Winston woke up the next morning feeling better about life than he had in a long time. The past couple of years he'd been on an emotional freight train that had imploded. His fiancée of four years had cheated on him with a good friend and he was still trying to process the loss of both his friend and the woman he'd considered his everything. Now he was here in the town where he'd spent school breaks and summers with Gia and her family, who had always treated him like he was one of their own and things seemed to be looking up.

He whistled as he reached the shop and went in. The store was silent. No sign of Gia yet. If he didn't hear from her by noon, he'd grab lunch from Hope's Diner down the street and take it to her parents' house where she was staying.

There was a temporary card table and chairs set up in the front that acted as their workspace and Winston was hooking up his laptop when the mail carrier, an older tall slim man with unusually tan legs and arms waved at him, indicating he wanted to enter. Winston beckoned the man in and he stepped through the door.

"Mornin'," he called, flashing a toothy grin and speaking in a thick Kentucky accent. "Where's Miss Gia today?"

"I haven't heard from her yet, but she should be in shortly." He nodded at a small box in the man's hand. "You got a package that needs a signature?"

"Nah, next door," he held up a thin stack of letters, "these are for you. Tell Miss Gia I'll see her tomorrow. Damn shame what those old biddies are plotting...it's a wonder she's not sick with stress and worry."

Intrigued, Winston took the letters, mostly bills and junk mail, then placed them on the table. "Old biddies?"

"Yep. You're new in town, from Chicago, right?"

Staring, Winston said, "Yeah, how did you...?"

The man waved him off. "Small town. Everybody knows

everything round here. Anyway, there's a gaggle," he grinned, pleased with his own wit, "of retired busybodies with nothing better to do than gossip and stir up trouble. Now," he leaned in like he was about to share a juicy secret and Winston found himself leaning in too. "When Dillon Montgomery started the Santa shows, they were all up in arms fussing about the town's morality and such. Now that we've seen such a boon and Kissing Springs is flourishing, they act like it was their idea all along!" He harumphed for good measure. "That's why I'm happily divorced."

Winston held back a chuckle. So many characters in one place. He held out his hand. "I'm Winston Locke, by the way."

The old man had a surprisingly strong grip. "Name's Duke. I'm the mail carrier for the business district."

Winston wanted to ask if Duke was his last name or his first but he let the man continue.

"So, the committee's cause du jour is to preserve the town's manufacturing jobs, which are, for the most part, already gone. They want to block the tech firms from coming in by holding up their permits. The new robotics company announcement that they were building a large facility here was what started all this, then they heard what Miss Gia is planning to do with the printers and they think she's taking jobs from seamstresses and whatnot."

Winston's heart sank. He had no idea Gia's mission to help women feel good in their lingerie would be met with such resistance. "That's ridiculous," he said, shaking his head. "Gia's trying to innovate and bring new jobs to the town."

Duke nodded in agreement. "I know, son. But you know how it is. Change is hard for some people."

Winston sighed. "Yeah, I know. But Gia is determined to make this work. She's already invested so much time and money into this boutique, this is going to devastate her."

Duke patted Winston's arm. "Don't you worry, son. Sometimes it just takes a little time for people to come around. But I've got a feeling our girl is going to make it. I've known her since she was little and she's always been determined and resourceful."

Winston rested his elbows on the desk thinking about the older man's words. "Thanks, Duke. I hope you're right."

"Hopefully they'll find something else to be outraged about soon enough." Duke held up a finger. "Oh, wanted to tell you, some of the other men in town meet up at the bookstore once a month for our book club. You been to the Book Barrel yet?"

Winston frowned. "Book Barrel? No, not yet."

"Yeah, check it out, actually, the owner is a Mitchell too… nephew or a cousin, I think. Check it out. Tell Miss Gia to take you by there." Duke checked his watch. "Well, I gotta keep moving, see you tomorrow."

Duke saluted and left the store to continue his rounds.

Winston took a deep breath and tented his fingers feeling like he had been hit by a ton of bricks. He had to help his friend but how? As an IT project manager in Chicago, he had no experience in dealing with small-town politics or committees; he dealt with systems and processes.

Working with Gia to get her store up and running was a new, unexplored frontier for Winston. When she'd contacted him with her plan and asked if he'd be interested in helping her as a contractor, Winston had jumped at the chance. He was in between projects anyway, might as well take some time out to help a friend in need.

Speaking of Gia, she should have been in by now. He checked his watch, verifying that it was nearly noon. With a sense of dread, Winston pulled out his phone and dialed Gia's number. After a few rings, a deep male voice answered.

Pulling the phone from his ear, he stared at it as if it would provide answers. "What the hell are you doing with Gia's phone?" Winston barked, unable to hide his anger.

Dre's voice was tense, but Winston could sense the underlying irritation. "I saw your name and figured you'd want to know Gia's in the hospital. Her appendix ruptured and she's recovering from surgery right now."

Winston's heart stopped and the anger seeped out of him. "Oh my God. Is she okay?"

"Yeah, she's in good hands. They caught it early enough, but she'll need a few days to recover."

Winston's mind raced. He needed to be there for her. He should be there, not Dre. "I'm on my way to the hospital. Which one is it?"

Dre hesitated before answering, "We're in Louisville at Norton but the doctor said she's going to be out of it for the next few hours. You might as well come tomorrow."

Why did Dre, of all people, have more information than he did? "Where's her family? Why are you there?"

Dre sighed. "Her parents are on a cruise and Jameson has a sick baby to look after. I was with her when she started feeling sick last night and I took her to the emergency room."

He ran a hand over his face. Well, that confirmed Dre's earlier boast that he had plans with her. She spent the night with him, even though she'd insisted to him it was a one-night thing.

Winston's frustration flared as he realized the gravity of the situation. He needed to be there for Gia but couldn't see past his issues with Dre. "Okay, I'll call her tomorrow."

He hung up the phone. As Winston closed up the store for the day, , he couldn't shake the feeling of helplessness. Gia was in the hospital and he was miles away, unable to do anything but wait. He knew he had to be there for her, but he couldn't shake the anger he felt towards Dre. It wasn't just jealousy anymore; it was a deep-seated resentment.

Once he was home, Winston looked around the house he was renting. He needed to distract himself, find something to take his mind off the situation. He could start with researching Kissing Springs. The more he knew about this town, the better. Then he could dig into his true mission.

Know thy enemy.

Turning to his laptop, Winston got to work. Within seconds, he had plenty of results.

He got up and used the small coffee maker in the kitchen to make a fresh cup of coffee. As he sipped, he scrolled through pages of social media profiles, looking for anything that could help him. And then he found it.

Winston's blood boiled. This was the guy Gia couldn't resist?

He saved the info and made a plan. He would wait until Gia was feeling better, and then he would tell her what he found. In the meantime, he'd handle the old biddies as well.

Surely, once she saw the real Dre, she would realize he wasn't the right person for her. Winston felt a sickening sensation in his stomach, but he couldn't stop himself. His jealousy had taken over, and he was determined to get what he wanted.

CHAPTER 5
Gia

Gia woke, groggy and confused. She blinked slowly, taking in her surroundings. As Gia's vision cleared, she realized she was lying in a hospital bed. The room was sterile and smelled of disinfectant. The view from the window was of a dreary, gray day outside. Gia's head throbbed with pain, and she couldn't remember how she had gotten there.

She rubbed her eyes trying to piece together what had happened. Memories of the previous day came flooding back, and she groaned softly as dull, throbbing pain coursed through her body. She turned her head to the side, her eyes widening as she saw Dre slumped over in a chair, his eyes closed, his breathing deep and steady.

How long had he been sitting at her side? She knew he was the one who had driven her here. What happened? She remembered seeing him rehearse at the theater then he invited her over to tell her the townspeople were fighting against technology, then she recalled being angry, but wasn't sure why.

Another memory hit her as she ran her tongue over her teeth. She'd thrown up. Her mouth was sour with faint remnants of bile.

Gia felt a pang of embarrassment. She had always been fiercely independent, and the thought that Dre took care of her made her feel helpless. She tried to sit up, but a sharp stab of pain shot through her abdomen, and she gasped, biting down on her lip to keep from crying out.

Dre stirred, his eyes flickering open as he sat up straighter, a look of concern crossing his face. "Hey," he said softly. "You're awake."

Gia looked away, attempting to shift her body so that her back was to him but pain forced her to stay still. She didn't want him to see her like this, weak and vulnerable.

Wishing she could brush her teeth, Gia licked her lips. "Dre, what are you doing here?" She cleared her throat, trying to make her voice sound stronger than it was.

"The nurse said I could stay," he motioned to the uncomfortable looking chair under him, "so I camped out. You feeling ok? Or as well as can be expected?"

Gia looked down at the sheets, her hands twisting together nervously. "I'm fine," she lied. "You didn't have to stay."

Dre's expression turned serious as he leaned forward. "Gia, you passed out in my living room. You could've been seriously hurt if I hadn't been there to help you. I just wanted to make sure you were all right."

Gia bit her lip, feeling guilt wash over her. She'd been so caught up in all the things she needed to do that she'd ignored the increasing pain in her body. "I didn't mean to burden you."

Dre looked like he wanted to take her hand but he stayed still. "You're not a burden." He cleared his throat. "And you have every right to be angry and creeped out about my news alerts...I swear, I was just curious about the stuff that happened to you last year. I'm not stalking you or anything, I just thought you got a raw deal. I deleted that alert."

A raw deal was putting it lightly. Her former partner had stolen her ideas, and then sued her for ownership of the company they created together. Thinking about that mess made her pain worse and she struggled to keep from wincing. She needed to focus on something else.

"Why did you really move to Kissing Springs?" The question nagged at her.

He was silent for a beat, then his shoulders slumped. "Most of what I told you is true. I heard that Derby Nights paid well and I decided to check it out." Dre ran a hand over his head and Gia could tell he was struggling with whatever he needed to say.

"A few nights after I met you, a woman approached me after our show, telling me that she was an event planner and she coordinated a lot of destination bachelorette parties for brides coming to Nashville. She had one coming up that would be held at an exclusive estate and she was looking for a single dancer. I was fine with that; I've done private parties before, and the money tends to be great. So, she says come up to my hotel suite, let's have a drink and work out details. Not my first rodeo; I know what this is, so I go."

He stopped, shifting in his seat. Gia held her breath, waiting for him to continue.

Looking down at his hands, he said, "I will spare you the details, but I woke up in her bed wearing nothing but a condom. She'd emptied my wallet and was long gone."

Speechless, Gia looked up at him, her eyes meeting his.

"You're the second person I've told. I had to call my best friend Darius to help me, so he knows, but I didn't report the assault and I don't intend to. I tried to get back to normal, but I realized that I needed to get out of Nashville. Darius told me about Kissing Springs and Derby Nights."

"She drugged your drink?"

He nodded. "The last thing I remember is her refilling my glass and telling me to sit on the bed."

Gia couldn't imagine what he'd gone through. And now she'd pushed him to relive what might have been the worst experience of his life. "Dre, I'm so sorry, I didn't know..."

"Of course, you didn't know, but I get why you were

suspicious of my move here. I know how this looks and that's why I told you. I wanted to reassure you."

She forgot about her vulnerability and embarrassment as the urge to comfort him overwhelmed her. A warmth spread through her chest. The man had, she realized with clarity, saved her life. And was trying to make sure she felt safe with him.

He looked like he'd just spent an uncomfortable night dozing in a hospital chair, but he was there. What was she supposed to do with that information?

No longer able to meet his gaze, she studied her hands. "I'm glad you trusted me enough to share."

"I figured you needed to know the whole story, even if that meant you think less of me," he said, his gaze shifting to the window.

She frowned. "I don't think any less of you. To me, you've done what you felt was needed for you to move forward. And maybe," she shrugged. "we've crossed paths again for a reason."

Dre turned back to her and Gia could see the concern in his eyes but there was something else there messing with her mind. Affection? Desire? She tucked that away for another time.

Breaking their eye contact, Gia ran her fingers over the bleach scented white sheet covering her as an awkward silence settled over them.

Finally, Dre stood. "Well, I should probably get going. Winston called while you were asleep, I think he's planning to come see you today."

As much as she needed time alone to process everything that had gone on, she didn't want him to go yet. "I feel like I keep saying thank you...I'm usually not this...needy," she trailed off. "I should probably put you on payroll."

Her attempt to lighten the mood was met with silence as Dre stared out the window, avoiding her gaze. "No need. I have a job already."

"I didn't mean it like that, I was joking," she said.

"No worries," he motioned to the door, "I'm gonna head out."

Before she could decide if she wanted to stall him again, the door to Gia's room opened, and a middle-aged woman in a white coat stepped in. "Ah, I see you're awake," the doctor said with a smile as she walked over to the bed. She motioned to Dre. "I'm Dr. Lindsey, no need to leave just yet, you'll need to hear this."

Gia watched as Dre hovered awkwardly while the doctor checked her vitals and made some notes on her tablet. "How are you feeling?" the doctor asked.

Gia winced as she shifted on the bed. "Better than yesterday, I guess."

The doctor nodded. "Good. We ran some tests, and everything looks fine. You can go home today, but you'll need to be under someone's care for the next week."

Gia frowned. "What do you mean?"

"I mean that you shouldn't be alone for the next seven days," the doctor explained. "You had some complications during the surgery, and we want to make sure you're okay."

Dre stepped forward, his eyes meeting hers. "I can take care of her," he said.

Dr. Lindsey looked between Dre and Gia, then nodded. "Good, I'll have the nurse brief you on what needs to be done and we'll want to have her in for a follow up in ten days." She turned to Gia, "Is this your...husband?"

Gia's eyes widened and she opened her mouth to protest, but Dre spoke up before she could. "No, I'm just a friend."

The doctor raised an eyebrow but didn't say anything else. "Right. Well, as long as someone is with her at all times, she should be fine. I'll go ahead and release her to your care."

She glanced at the tablet in her hand. "I'll send the nurse in with her discharge instructions and we'll send her prescriptions to the pharmacy. Make sure she takes all of her medication." She turned to Gia, "You'll need to take it easy for a few days. No strenuous activity."

Dre nodded. "Thank you, Dr. Lindsey."

The doctor gave them one last smile before walking out of the room. Gia sank back into the pillows, feeling a mix of relief and anxiety. She didn't want to be a burden on Dre, but she also didn't want to be alone right now.

She regarded Dre. What would happen after they spent a week together confined to his small apartment while he took care of her? Any attraction he felt for her was probably long gone. She was here in the hospital after vomiting in the man's sink and bathroom then passing out.

Raising a trembling hand to her head she realized her wash and go style had long gone; her hair was a mess but there was nothing to be done about it right then. She felt like she'd been run over by a herd of buffalo.

Why had he agreed to take care of her?

Once the week was over, he'd probably be glad to get back to his carefree single life. She would continue her not so carefree life and they might see each other around town, which she should have been ok with but she frowned. Why did that bother her so much?

All the questions running through her were exhausting.

"The week will go by fast," she said suddenly, "then I'll be out of your hair."

Dre scowled, his eyes searching hers. "What are you talking about?"

Gia shrugged, trying to play it cool. "Just...I don't want to be a burden on you. I know you have your own life to live."

Dre's eyes bored into hers. "You're not a burden, Gia," he said. "I told your doctor I'd handle your care and that's what I'm doing. So that's that. We good?"

Gia felt her heart flutter in her chest. This wasn't going to work. "You don't have to do this," she said, her voice slightly above a whisper. "We barely know each other. I'll ask Winston if I can stay with him."

Dre's eyes darkened, and he leaned in close to her. "No," he said, his voice low and commanding. "I think Winston should handle the business stuff since he knows more about it. You can have my room; I'll stay in the guest bedroom, and you can take it easy, focus on recovering as she told you to do. End of discussion."

The man had a point. Winston would hover and fuss over her like an anxious new mother and she didn't want that. She wasn't sure what kind of caretaker Dre would be, but she didn't get a sense that he was the type to be overbearing. She guessed she'd find out soon enough.

Gia's breath caught in her throat as she looked into Dre's intense gaze. There was something there, something that made her pulse race and her body tingle with anticipation.

She noted in the paperwork the nurse gave them that Dr. Lindsey's 'no strenuous activity' rule included sex. She'd wanted to ask exactly how long she was expected to go without but refused to do so in front of Dre.

She couldn't deny the attraction she felt for him, but she didn't want to complicate things even further. She needed to focus on getting her strength back and getting her business off the ground.

"Hmm. You gonna be this bossy all week?" she asked, only half joking.

Dre lifted a shoulder. "Depends. Are you going to actually take it easy? I get the sense you don't do well with being still."

Of course, she didn't. Gia rolled her eyes but couldn't help the smile that tugged at the corners of her mouth. "I can be still," she said, although as she spoke the words, she wasn't entirely sure she could. "But you have to promise not to treat me like a delicate flower. I'm not going to break."

Dre smirked. "I never thought you were delicate," he said. "But I'll try to hold back on the bossiness, as long as you promise to listen to me when I tell you to rest."

Gia nodded. Maybe, just maybe, they could get through this without things getting even more complicated.

As Dre helped her get dressed and gather her things, Gia

couldn't help but steal glances at him, taking in the way his muscles flexed beneath his shirt and the way his eyes crinkled when he smiled. Yep, resisting him was going to take all the willpower she had.

They made their way out of the hospital and into Dre's car, and Gia leaned back in the passenger seat, feeling a wave of exhaustion wash over her, but she couldn't rest just yet. "Can we stop at my parents' house to get my suitcase?"

He glanced at her. "You sure you're up for packing? You sound like you're barely holding on."

"It's not as much effort as you think. I've kinda been living out of my suitcases since I moved back. I figured I'd have my own place by now...but hell, I also assumed I'd be a successful lingerie designer showing at fashion weeks around the world, not starting over in my podunk hometown that I couldn't wait to get out of after high school." She leaned against the car window. That short speech had exhausted her and the thought of lugging her suitcase out of her bedroom to Dre's trunk made her want to curl up in the back seat.

Dre put a hand on her shoulder, giving it a gentle squeeze. "Hey. You'll get there, Gia. You're strong, and you're talented. It's just a matter of time before you get back on your feet."

Gia looked at Dre. He was right. She was strong, and she could do this.

They made their way to Gia's parents' house, and Gia packed her suitcase and a few other items before they headed back to Dre's apartment. As they entered the small space, Gia recalled the last time she was there. She'd been so angry and disappointed that he'd dug into her life online and now, it seemed so insignificant compared to what he'd done, was doing, to help her. She'd have to figure out some kind of way to repay him.

Dre led her to the couch and handed her a pillow and blanket. "You rest here," he said, "I'll make us some food."

Gia nodded, propping herself up on the pillow he'd left for her. It smelled faintly of him and she allowed herself to inhale a bit, enjoying the sensation. As Dre disappeared into the kitchen, she couldn't help but let her mind wander. She had been so focused on her career that she had forgotten what it was like to have someone take care of her. She had always been the one taking care of herself, and now Dre was here, giving her the support she needed.

She closed her eyes, feeling the weight of exhaustion take over. What seemed like only a few minutes later, Dre nudged her as he set a tv tray in front of her.

Gia sat up, examining the food he'd placed on the tray. There was a dark green leafy salad and a bowl of chicken noodle soup along with a tall glass of water.

"Hey," he said, smiling at her. "You ready to eat and take your pills?" He pointed at the salad. "That's a kale and apple salad with a lemon vinaigrette but if you're not into kale, there's chicken noodle soup."

Gia took a forkful of the salad, then another. She hadn't realized how hungry she was until now. "Thanks, I love kale," she said, crunching on the apple chunks. "This is really good."

Dre grinned, looking pleased with himself. "I'm glad you like it."

As they ate in comfortable silence, Gia glanced up at him, taking in his chiseled jawline and full lips. She knew what those lips felt like on hers and wanted to taste him again, to feel his body pressed against her. The thought made her heart race.

Nope. She grabbed the water, taking a big swig. Beyond her doctor's orders, there were a million reasons why she shouldn't be thinking such things.

Dre caught her staring and gave her a quizzical look. "What's on your mind?"

Gia shook her head, shoving her NSFW thoughts away. "Nothing," she said, polishing off the salad, "This was like the best salad I've had in a long time...you cook?"

"Not really. I can do basics, but that soup came from the can."

"I imagine you treat your body like a shrine and don't eat junk food." She glanced at his abs with envy. There probably wasn't an ounce of fat on him.

He smirked. "Every now and then, I'll treat myself to fast food fries, that's my weakness, but yeah, I have to eat right or else. So, there's plenty of protein and vegetables in the kitchen."

She glanced at him again, imagining him doing push-ups while she lay under him. Lord, help her, this was going to be a long week. She sighed out loud.

"What's up, you need a pain pill?" he asked, his face full of concern.

"No, I'm fine," she said quickly.

Dre didn't look convinced, but he didn't push the issue. They finished their meal in silence, and Dre helped Gia get comfortable on the couch.

"I want my laptop, but I should check in with my family first, see how my nephew is doing," she said, as her eyes drooped. What she really wanted was to take a quick power nap.

"Yeah, your brother called while you were asleep. You want to call him back after your nap?"

"Who said I need another nap?" she said over a yawn. "I'm good, I'm gonna close my eyes for just a second then I'll call."

She drifted off.

CHAPTER 6

Dre busied himself by getting the spare room to setup as a bedroom. He had an old air mattress he'd gotten to tide him over while he waited for his bed to arrive when he'd first moved to Nashville. It was fairly comfortable; he'd make do for the few days Gia was recovering.

Once the mattress was inflated, he strode into the living room to check on Gia, assuming she was still asleep.

She was stretched out on her left side with his blanket tucked under her, snoring softly. She looked at peace but as he leaned in, he frowned. She had a thin layer of sweat on her forehead. He laid the back of his hand gently against her cheek, checking for a fever. Her skin was warmer than expected and he rose to grab a cool face towel to dab on her skin.

He was pacing the room, debating on whether he should wake her and stick a thermometer in her mouth when Dre heard her phone buzz. He'd placed Gia's cell phone on a charger on the kitchen counter. Dre looked at the screen and saw that it was her brother Jameson. Did he know where Gia was? He had to be worried by now. Dre started to answer the phone but then he recalled Winston's aggressive response the last time he'd answered her phone. He left the phone where it was. He'd left his contact info with Jameson when they met up. Dre assumed Jameson would eventually get in touch.

As if on cue, Dre's cell phone rang. Eyeing the screen, Dre exhaled and braced himself. "What's up, Jameson."

He glanced over at Gia. He'd take her temperature in a bit.

"What's going on with you and my baby sister? Why is she at your place?" Jameson's voice was deep and tense.

Dre didn't want to wake Gia. "The doctor said she couldn't be alone for the next week while she recovers," he kept his voice low. "I was at the hospital with her, so I told the doctor I'd make sure she was ok. I know you have a sick baby to take care of and your parents are out of town. That's it."

"How are you the one at the hospital with her? You two barely knew each other. Where is she? Put her on the phone." Jameson's words were aggressive but Dre could hear the panic beneath the surface. He, however, would do what was in Gia's best interest and that meant letting her get her rest.

Dre shook his head. "She's sleeping. The meds they have her on cause drowsiness, plus I think she's in more pain than she lets on and she needs the downtime. I'll have her call you when she's up."

"Are you sure she's ok? I'd be over there now but my son is sick, and I don't want to risk Gia catching anything, I'm staying away," the unsaid words were clear: *I don't trust you.* "Have her call the minute she's awake." The aggressive tone lightened. "Take care of her."

Dre nodded, even though Jameson couldn't see him. "I will. She's in good hands."

After they hung up, Dre turned to see Gia stirring awake. "Hey, sleepyhead," he said, "please call your brother before he sends a search party over here to string me up."

Gia sat up, rolling her eyes. "I take it he called you after he couldn't reach me. Don't mind him. He's mostly bark and no bite. You'd think he was my father."

Dre would have to take her word for that. Jameson sounded like he was ready to come rescue his sister at any moment. "He said we barely knew each other...I didn't want to get into any of that. But I get it. He's worried."

"I know. I should call him back." Gia's words were slightly slurred from grogginess.

Dre took her phone off the charger and handed it to her. "Go ahead. I'm going to finish getting my room ready for you."

As Gia talked to her brother, telling him about her surgery and reassuring him she wasn't in danger, Dre busied himself stripping the bed and putting fresh sheets on it. He didn't want to eavesdrop on her conversation, but he couldn't help but overhear bits and pieces.

Once the bed was done, Dre entered the living room where Gia was finishing her call. "Yep, I will. Thank you. Kiss my nephew for me."

"I've calmed him down. No mob will storm the building now," she said, smiling at him. "I gave him more detail than he wanted about our first meeting and that shut him up."

Dre's head shot up. "What exactly did you tell him about that?" Their first meeting had occurred when Gia and her friend visited the Nashville strip club that formerly employed him.

"That since your head's been between my thighs, we are pretty much past the getting to know you stage."

Shaking his head, Dre gathered up the dirty sheets and stuck them in a laundry basket. As he approached the small laundry closet off his bedroom, he feared that was all Gia thought of him, which he should have been ok with, but somehow, he realized, he'd slipped up and gone down this path where he might want more.

When Dre saw her in the audience that night in Nashville during his performance, he couldn't take his eyes off her. She'd had her curly cinnamon colored hair in a high bun and the rose gold sequined minidress she wore showed off her shapely legs as she stood clapping and cheering the dancers on. There was a point in their routines where the dancers would select willing members of the crowd to come on stage where they would receive a rose. Dre knew he was going to choose her and when she agreed to come on stage, he'd taken her hand and felt something shift in him.

Dre couldn't deny that he was attracted to Gia from the moment he saw her that night in Nashville. He had been performing for years, but there was something about her that was different. As he took her hand to lead her to the stage, he felt a spark, a connection that he couldn't explain.

After the show, he found himself hoping she'd stayed after for pictures with the dancers. He played it cool when he spotted her in line and while they chatted during the photo session. Then he'd offered to see her back to her hotel room when her friend Erika said she was going dancing and to his surprise, she'd invited him up.

Seeing her again in the restaurant and having his mother introduce Gia as her mentee had him shook. He'd never expected to run into his one-night stand again, yet there she was, looking just as shocked as he was. He immediately grabbed her hand and introduced himself hoping she would play along. He didn't want to explain to his mother how he knew her as that would inevitably lead to more questions about his current line of work. Dre had no intention of having that conversation with her in front of Gia and her male friend.

He'd sized up Winston immediately. The adoring glances, the closeness, and the small touches every chance he got. That man wanted more from Gia. But Gia was glancing at him every time he glanced at her.

Dre knew that she didn't feel the same way about him. Those looks were probably more surprise at seeing him than anything. He stuffed the sheets in the washer and added soap to the dispenser then pushed the button to start the cycle.

He'd revealed his darkest secret to Gia and she hadn't shamed him or pressed him to report what happened to law enforcement. She seemed to listen without judgment and he appreciated that more than she could ever know.

He let out a long breath. They would be spending a lot of time together this week; maybe he'd find she was spoiled and insufferable and he could move on once she went back to her parents' house.

That settled, Dre returned to the living room. Gia watched him intently. "So... are you thinking you regret letting a near stranger that you had sex with stay in your personal space for a week yet?" she said with a smile.

He chuckled, taking a seat in the arm chair beside the sofa. "No. Honestly, I was thinking I need to take time to fully unpack my stuff since I'm planning to stay for a while. And that maybe I should have gotten a bigger place. Your mind reading skills are rusty after your surgery, I'm guessing?"

"More like non-existent even before the surgery." She tilted her head, keeping her gaze locked on his. "So, since we're stuck with each other, I'm curious to know why your mother doesn't know what you actually do for a living."

He lifted a hand to his chin. "Because she will think I'm doing it as a cry for attention and she'll want to throw money at the problem like she always does which means she'll try to buy Derby Nights for me so that I can run it, which I don't want to do." He paused, deciding to be real with her. "I generally don't tell people who my mother is. I don't want them to treat me differently because of it. So I keep all of it under wraps." He took a breath. His complicated relationship with Skye was something he didn't want to get into right then. "So, I take it you enjoyed our one night?"

She rolled her eyes. "You know I did. Hell, everyone in the hotel that night probably knows I did."

He gave her a half grin. "Too bad you have to recover."

She was staring at his mouth, her lips parted. "Yep, too bad."

Her gaze shifted to his chest and he felt like crossing his arms to cover himself. He was used to women at the shows ogling him like a piece of prime rib; that was his job and he knew the more they looked, the better the tips were. But this was different. Her heated look seared a path straight to his groin. Dre forced his thoughts back to the doctor's warning.

"Wow. You want to put my clothes back on?" He lifted a brow at her.

Gia blinked, a wry grin on her face. "Huh...I guess that wasn't as subtle as I thought. I need to work on my poker face."

He chuckled. "Yeah, you do."

Dre got up from the chair, needing to occupy his hands before he said or did something foolish. The air between them was charged with something he couldn't quite identify, but he knew it was dangerous. "You want a cup of tea?" he asked, retreating to the kitchen.

"Yes, but I need the bathroom first."

Dre heard the strain in her voice as she got up.

"If you give me a second, I can help you stand up without straining yourself," he called.

"No, I'm ok. Be right back," she called back.

He heard her shuffle slowly toward the hallway. She was trying to put on the bravest face she could, he knew.

When he brought the steaming cups of tea out and set them on the table, she was back on the couch, the blanket he'd given her covering the lower half of her body.

"Thanks for the tea," she said, gingerly reaching for the cup. "So, what's your work schedule? I know you rehearse during the day."

He sipped his tea. "Since summer is considered off-season, we do shows Thursday through Saturday and then whatever private appearances we have booked."

Gia nodded. "Ok so I assume since it's Monday, you're off tonight?"

"Yep. I can keep a close eye on you for the next three nights, then I imagine your family will want you with them?"

Gia shook her head. "My parents are gone until Sunday. They're cruising the Mediterranean this week: I believe they are either in Mykonos or Santorini today. Or possibly Turkey, not sure which."

He placed his tea back on the table. He should have added a shot of something to it. "It's beautiful over there. I've been to Athens once to visit my father, who's Greek."

"You see him much?"

Dre shook his head. "He sent for us when I was about five. He wanted my mom to retire from modeling and move to Greece with him. She wasn't having it. He said she was on her own if she didn't stay and that was that."

Gia gripped her tea with both hands as she sipped. "Can I ask you something personal, well, more personal than my other invasive questions?"

"You can ask but I reserve the right to not answer."

She sipped her tea. "Fair. How are you dealing with...what happened to you?"

He thought about her question for a moment then said, "It's made me change my behavior. No more hotel rooms with women I just met, for one."

He drummed his fingers on his leg. "I saw this post online recently about the girlfriend code where it lays out how women support each other when they're going out at night, you know what I'm talking about?"

Gia nodded. "You don't let your friend leave with some random man, you ensure only the bartender handles your drinks, etc."

"Yep. I thought about that and how women have to be so careful...before my incident, I wouldn't have even finished the post because that had nothing to do with me, but now, I realize how important it is." He gripped his cup but didn't drink from it.

"How that practice has probably saved a lot of women from being victims..." He glanced up at her. "According to girlfriend code, your friend shouldn't have let you leave with me."

"Well, to be fair, she assumed you were just making sure I got into the limo she hired. So, in her mind, the risk was low that something bad would have happened to me, but she also asked your coworker about you and he vouched for you," she said. "We look out for each other in our own way."

Dre remembered seeing Gia's friend deep in conversation with his fellow dancer. He hadn't mentioned her inquiries to him.

"I'm glad you've got someone looking out for you," he said, realizing that he envied her that. He had very few people doing the same for him.

Gia nodded slowly. "For what it's worth, you can count on me to look out for you, too. Can't do much in my present state, but you get the idea."

She could still turn out to be spoiled and insufferable, he decided. But right now, he wanted to hug her.

She sighed, set the tea down, then leaned back into the couch cushions. "Anyway, it's only eight and I don't want to go to sleep for the night so early. You ok with watching a movie?"

Before he could respond, her phone vibrated on the table, causing their cups to shake.

Gia slid the phone over. "It's Winston. Let me take this." She looked at him.

Did that mean she wanted privacy to talk to him? "I'll go in the other room if you..."

"No, you're fine." She waved her hand slightly indicating he could stay.

Dre watched her answer the phone and couldn't help but notice how her entire demeanor changed. She sat up straighter and her voice grew softer, like she was talking to a lover. He tried to ignore the conversation happening next to him, but he couldn't help hearing her intimate tone with Winston. She smiled softly as she spoke to him.

Dre got up from the chair to reheat his tea.

She told him they were only friends. Clearly Winston wanted more. Maybe Gia did too but wasn't ready to acknowledge her feelings yet.

He took a deep breath, putting his tea cup in the microwave. The sound drowned out Gia's conversation as Dre tried to shake off the sudden wave of sadness that washed over him.

He carried the steaming mug back to the living room as Gia was ending the conversation.

"Thank you, Winston, I don't know what I'd do without you." She ended the call, placing the phone back on the coffee table.

"What movie do you want to watch?" he asked, trying to sound nonchalant.

Gia looked up like she hadn't realized he was back in the room. "Winston just told me the same thing you did. He heard from Duke that there's an active effort to block anything tech from coming to town."

"Who's Duke?" Dre frowned.

"That's the mail man. He's a family friend." She sat up with effort, exhaling heavily. "I need my laptop. If both of you are hearing the same thing, there's bound to be some truth to the rumors." She closed her eyes. "I really wish the mayor was in town. I need to plead my case."

Dre could tell she was about to work herself into a frenzy. Placing a steadying hand on her shoulder, he attempted to calm her. "It's almost nine o'clock, there's nothing you can do about any of this right now. Worrying and stressing won't help."

Gia turned to face him, eyes wide and searching his face. "What if it's true? What if I can't get the store off the ground because the town won't evolve? If this all falls apart, it's one hundred percent my fault. I can't fail again."

Dre felt her worry and desperation and knew she was struggling to keep it together.

She rubbed her arms. "What am I going to do if this doesn't

work? I brought Winston in to help me with the technology, I need to pay him for his time, your mother is investing in the store and she's going to want a good return on her money. All of these people helped me because they believed in me, but what if they're wrong?"

He took a seat on the edge of the couch and placed a reassuring arm around her shoulders. "You won't fail. Everyone who believes in you knows you're smart and resourceful. You'll find a way to make it work, even if it means changing your strategy. Between the three of us, we'll figure something out, but you have to give yourself time to recover."

She pulled back. "I know...Winston said there's a public hearing meeting this week that he's going to attend to see what he can find out."

"Ok, good, so first thing tomorrow, we can figure out a plan of action. But tonight, you should rest. You just had surgery and your body needs to heal so finish your tea and pick a movie."

Gia blinked at him for a moment. He saw the protest flare, but she relented, leaning back against the sofa cushion. "Ok, I should allow my body to begin healing," she said, almost as a mantra. She glanced at him, "Maybe I'll just check my email and see..."

He crossed his arms deliberately and gave her a one brow raised stare. "Is checking your email a relaxing activity?"

Her shoulders slumped. "Ok...no email then."

Dre sensed he'd just won a major battle. "Well, that went better than I thought. I assumed I was going to have to pin you down to get you to relax."

Shrugging, she said, "Every fiber of me wants to grab that laptop and start working but deep down, I know you're right. I'm not at one hundred percent right now and the stress won't help. So, I'm forcing myself to relax. Plus, I'm in some pain," she admitted, "My mind wants to keep working but physically I'm kind of done."

Dre felt the defeat in her voice. "Hey, why don't I get you some water so you can take a pain pill while you find us a movie?" he asked, passing her the television remote control.

Gia nodded, a small smile tugging at her lips. "Yeah, let's do that."

CHAPTER 7

Winston

Winston nearly ran out into the blazing afternoon sun, a slight grin on his face as he walked out of the city hall building. He had convinced the board to approve Gia's building permits so that the renovation work could continue. It took some convincing, but he knew he had to make them see that this was a chance for their town to grow and, contrary to what the old biddies were saying, create jobs.

He'd outlined a plan to hire interns from the local high school and community college and teach them how to operate 3D printers which he could tell impressed the board. They'd wanted to know why Gia wasn't there and he told them she was recovering from surgery. He learned most of the members knew her family, but hadn't heard about her hospitalization.

The meeting had ended with everyone excited about the new venture and Winston couldn't wait to share the news with Gia.

Wanting to impress the board, Winston had opted to wear a sports coat to the hearing. Now that the meeting was over, he'd been way overdressed for the whole affair, he peeled the jacket off and wished he'd worn a golf shirt instead. He felt the sweat running down his back and knew he needed to go home and change into something more comfortable before he headed back to the store.

The house he'd rented for his stay was walking distance from the center of town and close to Love Lock Bridge, a popular tourist attraction where couples could attach locks to the iron metalwork symbolizing their love.

As he approached the sunny yellow house, Winston thought about the foster homes he'd shuffled through as a kid. He never settled in any one; none of them felt like home and he knew his stay would be temporary. He would have loved coming home to a house like this back then. This house looked like love and acceptance. There was a picket fence, several small windows that bathed the house in sunlight and a nice sized yard with vibrant blooms in a variety of colors. Love Lock Bridge was in the near distance, its silver locks glinting in the sunlight.

One day, he'd take Gia to visit the bridge, add their special lock and have a picnic lunch while they enjoyed the day.

By the time he unlocked the front door, he was drenched in sweat. Thankful for the cool air in the house, Winston dropped his keys and wallet on the kitchen table and headed toward the bedroom. He also needed to make some calls, but he would do that after his shower.

Once he'd showered and changed into a golf shirt and casual shorts, Winston called the contractors to let them know they could continue working. The task took longer than expected and by the time he was ready to call it a day, his stomach growled in complaint. Glancing at the time on his laptop, Winston saw that it was nearly six. He decided to head over to Hope's Diner and pick up something he could bring back to the house. He also still needed to call Gia.

Winston stepped into the diner. He'd eaten in the local restaurant a couple times before and each time he felt like he'd stepped into the past. The place reminded him of the old school diners he saw in movies: checkered floors, red booths, chrome trim, vintage signs, and a jukebox in the corner.

There was a small, horseshoe-shaped counter for patrons to sit at and Winston nodded to two older men that were grumbling about the heat as they shoveled food into their mouths.

The scents of bacon, burgers, and French fries wafted through the air.

He took a seat at the counter, greeting the older server, who wiped down a table. "Hey Winston! You keepin' cool in this heat?"

Winston chuckled. "Trying my best, but it's a losing battle. How about you?"

"Oh, I've seen worse, I grew up in Arizona," she replied with a grin. "What can I get you?"

"I'll have a cheeseburger and fries to go, please. And a slice of peach pie too," Winston added. He had been sticking to the meal plan Jameson laid out for him but tonight he was going to indulge a bit.

"You got it. Anything to drink?"

"Just water, thanks."

As he waited for his food, Winston glanced around at the other diners.

The man sitting closest to him nodded in greeting. "You're Winston, aren't you? Used to stay with Carla and Charlie? Gia's friend from school?"

Winston still couldn't get used to the small-town familiarity he encountered. "Yeah, I'm Winston."

"Thought so. I'm Joe," he motioned to the other man next to him. "That's Hank. The peach pie came from Minnie's Pie Shop. Best pies in the state if you ask me."

Hank grunted. "You better not let Liz hear you say that. She'll have your hide."

Joe turned to his friend. "You kidding me? Liz and Cherie didn't think twice about leaving us high and dry to go see those damn oily young boys at Derby Nights. So, I'm having a slice of peach pie." The older man groused, fanning himself with the newspaper in his hand.

Attempting to tune the men out, Winston pulled his phone out of his pocket and was scrolling through the news feed.

Joe continued to complain. "Yeah, you know if any of us had a retirement party at a strip club, all the women in town would be ready to tar and feather our asses. But they abandoned us cause Joyce wanted to go out in style."

Looking up from his phone, Winston turned to Joe. "What's this about a retirement party at the strip club?"

Joe was still pouting. Hank leaned in so he was facing Winston. "Our wives are at a retirement party for Joyce Paxton, she worked at the post office for thirty-five years, and Joyce decided she wanted to rent out Derby Nights for the evening."

"Those old birds are gonna come back tipsy and wanting attention later on," Joe predicted. "There's fresh meat they're drooling over. Like those young men want them."

Winston didn't know where to begin he had so many questions. A retirement party at Derby Nights? "Fresh meat?"

"Yeah, Joe says there's a new group of strippers. The women are losing their minds, especially over the green eyed one." Joe sighed. "So, we're here eating dinner cause our wives decided they weren't cooking tonight."

The wheels started turning as Winston drummed his fingers on the counter. They had to be talking about Dre, which meant he wouldn't be home that evening.

Maybe, he reasoned, she'd want to celebrate. Before he could talk himself out of it, Winston called Gia. "Hey, just calling to check on you, see if you needed anything."

"I'm doing ok. How did it go earlier?" She sounded tense.

"We got it," he said triumphantly. "The board approved the permits and the contractors can continue working."

"Oh my god, that's amazing! Thank you so much for doing that for me," Gia gushed. Winston noted that she sounded like she was doing much better.

"I told you I'd take care of it," Winston said with a smile. "I do have a few things to go over with you, you up for some company?"

"Sure, yeah, my caretaker had to go into work tonight so that would be good."

Winston clenched his fist in victory. Good, Dre was already gone. "Did you eat? I'm at Hope's Diner. I can get you something."

"I'd love some of their tomato soup if they have any left. Oh, and a grilled cheese sandwich."

"I'll check. Can you send me the address where you are? I'll be over soon."

"Bless you, you're the best."

Winston's heart leapt as soon as he saw the text with Dre's address. He motioned to the server and gave her Gia's order.

* * *

Winston pulled up to the small apartment complex and parked. There were four buildings that looked like they each held four units, two upstairs and two on the street level. Judging by the numbering, Dre's apartment was on the main level.

He grabbed the food and hurried to the door. Anticipation of seeing Gia had him starting to sweat and he willed himself to calm down. This was his best friend. He slowed his pace and took a deep breath as he knocked on the door.

"Win?" she called from the other side. "One second."

She opened the door, beaming at him. "Hey, sorry it took me a minute; I'm still moving a little slower than normal." She waved him in.

Gia was wearing a loose-fitting teal baby doll dress that flowed around her curves and stopped mid-thigh, exposing her bronzed shapely legs. Her feet were bare and her unruly curls were pulled back in a messy bun. She wore no makeup, but to Winston she looked stunning. He was sure that he wasn't the only one who thought so.

"So," he took in Dre's sparse apartment, noted the moving boxes stacked in the corner. "Not exactly the Ritz, huh? This place brings back memories of my first place after college."

Gia patted his shoulder. "I wish my first apartment after college was this big. That first place was my New York City reality check." She eyed the bag in his hand. "Can we eat? I can smell the grease and I've missed it."

Winston moved toward the kitchen. "I didn't think to ask, but is your diet restricted? Should you be eating grilled cheese?"

As soon as he placed the bag of food on the small dining table, Gia was tearing through it. "No restrictions but Dre's got me eating clean. God, that burger smells good." She snagged one of his fries, shoving it in her mouth like she hadn't eaten in days. "I'll grab some plates and stuff. You want a beer? We can eat out on the deck."

Winston helped her get the food onto plates and followed her through the master bedroom to a small balcony. He noticed the large bed was half made, as if only one person occupied it. He released a silent breath. Seeing the bed gave him hope they weren't sleeping together.

Gia unlocked the sliding door and pushed it open. There were two wicker chairs and a small round table on the deck, but Winston immediately saw why she wanted to sit there. The view of the sunset from their vantage point was breathtaking.

The sky was painted with brushstrokes of red, purple, and gold, with the sun slowly sinking into the horizon. Winston paused, unable to shift his gaze from the beauty before him. He sat down across from Gia. "I'll bet this is your favorite spot."

She dragged her spoon through her soup. "You know me so well. I've been sketching out here in the evenings."

"Good," he said, between burger bites. "How are things with your temporary roommate?"

Gia nibbled the grilled cheese sandwich. "It's been fine. I'm eating better than I ever have. I've watched shows and movies that I've been meaning to catch." She licked her fingers. "But I feel like

I should be doing more. Being idle has given me time to think of all the things I need to take care of and all the ideas I have that I want to explore. I've been really inspired these last few days."

He noticed she hadn't really answered his question.

"I wish you had come to stay with me. I would have taken care of you." Better than Dre ever could, he knew.

"I know you would have, but you're making sure the business moves forward." Gia dropped the sandwich back onto the plate and wiped her hands. "Do you know how much that means to me? Especially since you were able to represent us in front of the board today. I almost cried when you told me they finally approved our plans."

Winston couldn't help the pride that surged through him. "Yeah, so about that, in a rare moment of inspiration, I proposed that we could recruit interns from the high school and community college and train them on the printers. I know we'd talked about that in passing but I threw it in and they loved the idea."

"Yes, we'll definitely do that. Noemie's the guidance counselor at Nelson; she can help get the word out."

"That's your brother's new wife, isn't it?"

Gia nodded in confirmation. "Yes, she'll love the idea."

As they tossed additional ideas for their budding internship program, Winston's enthusiasm rose as Gia spoke. Her passion for the business was contagious and he was happy to be a part of the process.

Suddenly, Gia gripped his hand and Winston could tell she was on the brink of tears again. "Win, you're amazing, you know that? You got everything back on track and you brought me grilled cheese from Hope's Diner! I'm so glad you came to Kissing Springs."

He brought her hand to his lips. "Anything for you, my dear."

Winston longed to tell her how much he adored her but now wasn't the time.

She glanced up at him in surprise and Winston knew he

needed to change the subject. "So, when is your roommate due back? I'm sure he's not going to be pleased to see me here."

Gia released his hand. "I'm not sure. He said his normal work schedule is Thursday through Sunday. I think this was a special event so no telling when he'll be back. And you're fine. I mentioned that you were stopping by."

Winston felt a pang of jealousy at her words. She made it seem like they were a couple living together. "He's not trying anything?" he asked, trying to keep his tone casual.

Gia raised an eyebrow in confusion. "What do you mean?"

"I think you know what I mean," Winston gestured vaguely. "You're a beautiful woman in a vulnerable position. I just don't want him taking advantage of the situation."

Gia rolled her eyes. "Winston, my reputation isn't in jeopardy. Dre's been a wonderful caretaker. I wish he'd bring home fries and ice cream but other than that, he's been respectful." She picked up her sandwich, pulling off a small piece. "Did you know he's a classically trained dancer and pianist? He studied at Alvin Ailey."

She sounded thoroughly impressed, Winston realized as he glanced at Gia. He itched to say something snide about Dre's dance training but resisted. "Hmph...let me guess, he's written you a song."

She let out a laugh. "You sound like a jealous boyfriend now. No, he hasn't even played for me, but there's a piano in the other bedroom."

"I mean, at the end of the day, how well do you know this man? Wasn't he supposed to be a one and done thing?" Winston folded his arms.

Gia's shoulders slumped. "Yeah, it was, but he's the reason I'm alive right now."

Standing up, Gia strode to the railing. "And you're right, I'll admit I don't know much about him, and I was hesitant to move in for a week, but this was the best option at the time. Usually, I can get a sense of something being off with the people I deal with, and I haven't gotten that sense from Dre."

"I just don't think you should be so trusting. The fact that he moved here—to the same town as you so soon after he met you—is highly suspect," Winston's voice rose and he forced himself to calm down but he had to made Gia see reason. "God knows what he's up to. He could be here to sabotage your business. Hell, he could be the reason your permits got stalled."

Another thought occurred to him. "What if his mother sent him here to keep an eye on you? Isn't she one of your investors?"

Gia whipped around to face him; her eyes narrowed. "Where did this conspiracy theory of yours come from? That's ridiculous, Win, and you know it."

Winston knew he'd pushed too far. He didn't really believe Dre was spying for his mother, but he needed her to start questioning Dre's actions before it was too late. "Look, maybe that's not the case, but there's more to him than what he's led you to believe. You need to watch your back. I don't trust him, and you shouldn't either. Keep a close eye on him, Gia."

She put a finger up, ready to fire back at him when she froze, staring at something beyond him.

Winston turned to see Dre reaching for the patio door.

CHAPTER 8
Gia

Gia watched as Dre slid the door open. She couldn't read his expression, but she imagined this wasn't the scene he'd hoped for when he returned home. Why was he back so early? She glanced at the time on her phone, confirming her suspicion that it wasn't even nine o'clock yet. The night was still young.

She wondered briefly if he'd come back because of the text she'd sent telling him Winston was coming by.

"Hey, can I talk to you for a second?" Dre asked, his eyes straying to Winston for a split second then landing squarely on hers.

Winston pushed himself up from the chair. "I can go."

Dre held up a hand. "Give us a second." His tone held no room for argument.

Winston scowled then flopped back into the seat.

Gia scooped up their empty plates and trash. "Sure, I'll just throw this stuff away," she said as she stepped back into the bedroom.

Closing the patio door, Dre followed her as she made her way to the kitchen. Gia threw the paper plates out and busied herself tidying the small kitchen. She wasn't sure how much of Winston's ranting he heard but she wasn't ready to talk about it. "I thought you had a show tonight?"

"I did. I had to leave early," Dre paused, running a hand through his hair. "I just found out one of my best friends was in a motorcycle accident tonight. They don't think he's going to make it and his girlfriend is falling apart. I need to go see him."

Gia placed the wine glass she'd been holding into the dishwasher and turned to him. "Oh no, I'm so sorry to hear that."

Without thinking, she pulled him into a hug.

Gia felt him stiffen slightly before he relaxed into the embrace. Gia held onto him tightly, trying to offer comfort in any way she could.

After a few moments, Dre pulled away. "Thanks," he said, his voice thick with emotion.

"Of course," Gia replied softly. She could see the pain etched on his face and she wondered what she could do to help. "Do you need me to come with you?"

Dre shook his head, looking at her intently. "You still have a few days of recovery left. I think you should stay with Winston."

Gia frowned. "That's not necessary. I was planning to go back home tomorrow."

Dre's eyes flickered to the window briefly before returning to hers. "You shouldn't be alone. I can tell you're still in pain."

He placed a hand on her shoulder. "Please. This will be one less thing I have to worry about while I'm there."

Gia started to protest but his words coupled with the look on his face stopped her. He was hurting and now wasn't the time to add to his stress. She sighed, knowing Dre was right.

"Ok," she said finally. "I'll stay with Winston until you get back."

Dre stared down at her, his expression unreadable. Finally, he spoke in a low voice. "I hope I'm doing the right thing. I hope you're here when I get back."

Gia's heart pulsed. She knew what he was saying but she shouldn't commit to an answer. Encouraging him was a bad idea.

Despite these thoughts, she needed to touch him. Before she could stop herself, Gia took his cheek in her hand. "Call me if you need to talk."

He gave her a slight nod then turned away. She watched as Dre approached the sink, staring at nothing. She could tell his mind was miles away. She'd give him some time alone, she decided, and walked back out to the deck.

Taking in a deep breath of the cool night air, Gia let the evening's calm wash over her. The sun had fully set, leaving behind a deep indigo sky full of stars. Taking the seat next to Winston, she tried to tamp down her annoyance at his earlier assertions that she was too naïve around Dre, but she didn't want to argue with him anymore. Gia imagined they'd have plenty of time to do that while she stayed with him.

She would miss this place. Staying with Dre for the past few days had done wonders for her state of mind. She hadn't realized how stressed she was until she had to slow down. She knew her time with Winston wouldn't be as idyllic.

"He's leaving for Nashville in a bit. His friend was in a bad accident." Gia turned to Winston. "Is that offer to stay with you still on the table?"

"Of course. Whenever you're ready."

"Ok, I'm going to pack a bag."

Winston rose from his seat. "Take your time. I'll be in the car."

She watched Winston amble through the patio door and then turned back to the sky. As a kid, Gia would stare at the sky and make wishes on all the stars she could see. She hadn't understood the concept of the falling star. Now, as she sat musing, a star did fall and Gia closed her eyes.

She wished for clarity, for a sign telling her what to do next. She wished for peace, for the pain in her body and heart to subside. And, saving the most critical for last, she wished for Dre's friend to recover.

Gia rose from her seat on shaky legs as exhaustion hit her full on. She made her way back into the bedroom, feeling the weight of the day's events bearing down on her. She took a deep breath and focused on packing a few things to take with her to Winston's house. The sooner she packed, the closer she'd be to collapsing in Winston's guest room.

Taking in Dre's large comfy bed, Gia knew she'd miss that as well. While she'd spent all her nights in it alone, she'd had vivid fantasies of the two of them celebrating her recovery in that bed.

She could curl up in his bed right now. Turning back to her suitcase, Gia forced herself to focus.

She hesitated, looking at the large open suitcase in front of her.

Should she take her whole suitcase?

Gia had only a few more days before she was considered well enough to be on her own, but Dre was right, she was in more pain than she wanted to admit.

Gia's shoulders slumped as she realized she might need more than a week to recover.

Sitting with that thought had her reeling. If she couldn't make more strides to get the store open, she'd fall further behind schedule. Her savings would run out and she'd be worse off than she was before.

Gia stood slowly, holding her tender side as she rose, intending to find Dre and ask if he had a smaller bag she could borrow.

He appeared in the doorway.

Gia's breath caught in her throat at the sight of Dre standing there looking like a lost little boy. She knew he was hurting, and she wanted nothing more than to comfort him. Taking a step forward, Gia wrapped her arms around him, inhaling the clean, male scent of him she'd grown used to while she stayed in his apartment.

Dre clung to her, his solid body against hers. Gia held him, her hand running soothingly over his back as he murmured his thanks in her ear. She continued to touch him, reassuring him without words that she was there.

Eventually, Dre pulled away, taking a deep, shuddering breath. He looked down at her, his eyes moist with sorrow but there was something else there too, something that made Gia's heart race a little faster.

Before she could even process it, he leaned in and kissed her, his lips pressing against hers in a way that made her head spin. This time his kiss was more tender and filled with emotion that had Gia's heart galloping in her chest. She clung to him as something within her shifted.

Dre's hands ran over her and as he pulled her closer to him, she gasped in pain when he grabbed her waist.

He pulled away immediately, his green eyes blazing. "I forgot about your side...I'm sorry." He released her as his gaze roamed her body. "Did I hurt you?"

Gia blinked. She couldn't really answer just then. She was seconds from letting him do whatever he wanted to her, the hell with the doctor's orders, but she was still very sore and as much as she wanted him, it wasn't a good idea.

She realized he was still waiting for an answer. "I'm still sore, but I'm fine."

"You sure?" She nodded and he breathed a sigh of relief. "I got carried away," he said, rubbing his chin as if to erase the tension between them.

"Me too."

As they stared at each other, Gia felt the crackle of the sparks of attraction between them. Maybe, she mused, this time apart would allow things to cool off. Maybe the next time she saw Dre, she'd be rational and realize he was too young and she didn't want the inconvenience of a relationship.

She snorted internally. Yeah, and maybe hogs with wings would float through all those stars she'd wished on as a kid.

"Do you have a smaller bag I can borrow to put my stuff in?"

she asked, clearing her throat and stepping further away from him.

Dre nodded, his eyes still fixed on hers. "Yeah. I'll go grab it for you."

He stepped out of the bedroom, leaving Gia alone with her thoughts. She tried to ignore the way her heart was still racing, the way her body was still humming with the memory of his touch. She couldn't afford to get sidetracked by a relationship right now, especially not with everything she had going on. But damn, it was hard to resist Dre when he looked at her with those expressive green eyes of his.

He returned a moment later, holding out a dark blue gym bag. "This should work," he said, his voice a little more controlled now.

"Thanks," Gia said, taking the bag from him. "This is perfect."

Dre nodded, his eyes still holding hers. "So, you're leaving your luggage here?" he said, his voice low and intense.

She dragged her gaze away, glancing at her open suitcase on the floor. "If that's ok? I can take it if it will be in the way."

"No, that's ok, it will be fine here. I guess I should be packing too," he said, but he didn't move.

Gia nodded, suddenly realizing the implication. By leaving her luggage, she sent the message that she intended to return.

She was resolute. She'd be back. He might need her; she rationalized as she folded and rolled items to place in the duffle bag. He would need a friend and that's what she would be. The anticipation simmered in her of connecting with him on that level.

Dre ran a hand over his forehead and strode to the small walk-in closet. He returned, tossing a large duffle on the bed. "You all set?"

Gia nodded, already missing him.

He pulled Gia into his arms, mindful of her tender areas. "Make sure you take your meds...and remember, no strenuous activity." He placed a warm kiss on her forehead. "Save that for me."

Gia's eyes slid shut, her mind conjuring all kinds of naked strenuous activities for them. "Safe travels."

She carried the duffle using her left arm, making it awkward to heft onto her shoulder. She needed to leave before she convinced him to take her to Nashville with him. Gia turned back. "Text me when you get where you're going, let me know you made it ok."

As she approached Winston's car, her thoughts drifted to Winston's vehement assertions that she shouldn't trust Dre. He'd said it with confidence, as if he knew something she didn't.

She looked back at Dre's apartment. Dre stood, watching her from the door. He waved once then he was gone.

Winston opened the passenger door for Gia then dumped her bag in the trunk.

Gia placed her purse in her lap and settled into the passenger seat, closing the seatbelt around her.

"Ready? Do you want to stop and grab something to eat before we head in?" Winston said, starting the car.

"No, I'm still full from dinner." She was distracted and hoped he wasn't in a mood to discuss things. Gia stared out the passenger window as they worked their way through the streets of Kissing Springs.

"You seem like you have a lot on your mind. Wanna talk about it?"

"Not really." She sighed. "Remember when we met? Freshman year? Damn, that was twenty years ago," she mused. Where has the time gone? Back then, she thought she wanted to create the next Apple or Microsoft.

"Yeah, time has flown by. I remember you were all into coding and tech then all of a sudden you jumped into fashion design. I couldn't understand how you were able to completely shift gears like that," Winston said, giving her a sidelong glance.

"It was that Art Appreciation class I took as an elective. I needed one more class to be considered a full-time student and I picked that one since it fit my schedule and wasn't full." She turned to face him. "That class literally changed the course of my life. I didn't even know I was artistic at that point. I learned to sketch in that class."

"You know what I realized, Gia? When you do something, you don't do it half-ass…you're all in, balls to the wall."

"Balls to the wall, huh?" she chuckled. "I've never heard that in the fashion world before. But yeah, I guess that's accurate."

Arriving at his house, Winston turned into the driveway and killed the engine. "Yep. It's a guy thing. Anyway, I think you want to be like that in your love life as well but something happened. If I had to guess, I would say it was your former business partner screwing you over, and now you're terrified to jump in. Would that be accurate?"

Gia, thinking about the latest sketches she'd done for a future menswear line, froze at his words. She hadn't told anyone about what happened with her ex-business partner.

She kept her voice steady. "What makes you think he had something to do with my ability to love?" She crossed her arms, then uncrossed them, willing herself out of protective mode.

Winston laid a hand on her arm. "Let's go inside. I bought some bourbon from Lockland Distillery, you heard of it? We can sip on it and talk."

Nodding, Gia eased herself out of the car. Maybe it was time to let the whole story out. She knew Winston would listen without judgement. "We'll go to the screened in porch where there's more room."

Sighing at what she knew was a dig on Dre's small terrace, Gia stepped into the house, reliving the memories. The house Winston rented used to belong to a family with two girls around her age, and she'd spent summers running around their back yard, banging the door between the yard and the screened porch shut.

Gia wondered what had happened to the family. She knew the girls had gone away for college, maybe in the Pacific Northwest or California, she couldn't recall.

Her mother told her the house had gone into foreclosure and was now owned by some faceless corporation. The house had been furnished when Winston rented it and to Gia, the interior had no personality. Neutral, bland walls and furniture that looked like it had been purchased in bulk from one of the big warehouse stores in Louisville adorned the spaces.

She'd make an offer on the house if her lingerie store took off, she vowed as she slipped out of her sandals, leaving them by the door. The house would be perfect for her and she could breathe new life into it. Make the inside look as loved as the outside.

Winston dropped his keys and Gia's bag on the table and hustled through the dark house, turning on lights. "Go ahead, I'll grab us some glasses and the bottle," he called from the hallway.

"Will do. You got cheesecake or chocolate? Or better yet, chocolate cheesecake?" she asked.

"No, but there's a slice of peach pie in the fridge. Go sit, I'll heat it up for you. And before you ask, no, I have no ice cream for it."

Gia rolled her eyes at his ability to read her mind. The pie would be perfect with a little ice cream, but she supposed she couldn't be picky.

She made her way to the screened porch and stretched out on the wicker loveseat. While she appreciated everyone's concern, she was tired of being treated like she was fragile and easily broken.

Winston placed a heavy glass of bourbon in front of her and settled on the opposite end of the loveseat, lifting her legs, and placing her feet in his lap.

He peered at her toes. "Glad you started getting pedicures. Back in the day, your feet could have been registered as lethal weapons."

Scowling at him, Gia took a sip of her drink. "They weren't that bad. You just caught me on a bad day. And what's up with the inside of this house? From the outside, it looks like some little old lady who loves gardening lives here."

"That's cause this husband-and-wife team do the lawn

maintenance. The wife does the landscape design and maintains the garden. The company that owns the property furnished it with stuff they had from model houses. That's what the real estate agent told me."

"My mom said some holding company owns this place. You think they would sell it?"

Winston sipped his bourbon, his brow furrowed. "You're looking to buy a house here? I thought you were hell bound on moving back to New York once the store is successful?"

"I am, but I was thinking this might make a nice investment property and I could stay here when I come to town. Or my niece could live here when she's done with school." She rested a hand under her chin. The bourbon was excellent, pleasantly warming her insides as a ceiling fan blew cool air over her skin.

"I suppose at some point I want to own a house of my own. Not sure New York is the best option. I might want to slow down in a few years."

Winston gaped at her. "Either that's the liquor talking or your injury has you soul searching."

She tilted her head back and forth. "Yeah, being still for a few days has me reflecting. Dre even had me meditating the other day. It's like sitting there thinking about breathing has my creativity on high. I have a ton of ideas for new designs."

"Good. You needed to slow down. You ever thought about settling down?"

She didn't want to admit it, but she had. Since she'd been home and got to see up close how happy her brother Jameson and his wife were, she found herself wondering if she could see herself getting married. "Maybe," she said finally, glancing at him. "You were close...you think you want to venture down that road again?"

He rubbed her foot absently. "I mean, yeah, I want a family... always wanted to give a child what I never had."

"I think you'll make an excellent father," Gia paused, then said the first thing that popped into her head. "I don't know if I want kids. I might be a little too driven to succeed right now, but I'm also damn near forty, If I'm not ready for kids now, when will I be?" She asked this aloud, not expecting him to answer.

"You can still have kids after forty, can't you? You have some time." Winston increased the pressure on the ball of Gia's foot and she sighed happily. She loved Winston's foot rubs.

Unbidden, her mind meandered back to the night she spent with Dre in Nashville. He hadn't rubbed her feet; he'd seduced them with a chipped piece of ice and that magnificent mouth of his. The thought made her toes start to tingle.

Gia took another sip of the liquor. Down, girl. Dre was *not* settle down and start a family material. Even as she reassured herself that, an image of Dre setting breakfast down in front of her had her pause. He'd made a smoothie bowl for her, complete with chia seeds, which she'd never had, and star fruit. He might make some woman a great husband one day.

She was exploring why the thought of Dre as someone else's irritated her when Winston spoke.

"So, talk to me about your ex-partner? Was there something more than business going on?"

Gia took a deep breath, trying to steel herself for the conversation. "No, there was nothing more than business going on. At least not on my end," she said, her voice coming out in a bitter, sarcastic tone. "But apparently he had different ideas."

She wasn't ready to reveal it to Winston, but she had viewed her ex-business partner as the ideal mate: strong business sense and unwavering commitment to family. She'd placed him on this pedestal of what the perfect man looked like and held the men she met to his standard. While she would have never crossed that line with him, she found herself wanting someone just like him. Until everything went to hell. Now she no longer trusted her judgment.

Winston's grip on her foot tightened slightly, as if offering support. "What happened?" he asked softly.

Gia took another sip of her bourbon, feeling the warmth spread through her body. "I don't know if there's much to say," she said, trying to keep her voice steady. "We were supposed to be partners, but he started making decisions without consulting me. And when I did have an idea, it got shut down. I really wanted to explore menswear, but he said the market was too small. Then he started taking more and more control, until it felt like I was just along for the ride."

She paused, tasted the bourbon again before she continued. "And then, when I tried to assert myself, he accused me of being difficult and unprofessional. He eventually accused me of being in love with him," she finished, the last words coming out with more force than she intended. Her fists clenched. She wasn't as over the whole mess as she'd originally thought.

Winston's hand on her foot stilled. "What? That's ridiculous," he said, his voice incredulous.

Gia let out a bitter laugh. "His wife and I were good friends before everything went south, but apparently he told her I wanted more, that I was obsessed with him and she was no longer on my side. She eventually testified against me in court. The sad part is, I miss her friendship way more than I miss the business."

Her shoulders slumped. "He was very effective at destroying everything I loved. Then losing the court case was the last straw."

Winston shook his head as he listened to her story. "I'm so sorry, Gia. That's really rough."

"Yeah," she said softly, tracing the rim of her glass with her finger. "The last few years have been tough. But I'm trying to move on and focus on building my new brand."

"Good for you," Winston said, his thumb rubbing small circles on the arch of her foot. "You're a strong woman, Gia. You'll get through this."

She managed a small smile. "Thanks, Win. Most days I don't feel strong. Seems like for every step forward I make, I get knocked back three."

"Well, the board approval was a win today. So, if you do the math, that's like, what about ten steps?"

She grinned at him, raising her glass at him in a virtual toast.

They sat in comfortable silence for a few moments, the hum of the ceiling fan and the chirping of crickets outside the only sounds. It was nice to have someone who wasn't treating her like she was made of glass, who didn't tiptoe around her or try to fix her problems. Winston had always been a stabilizing presence in her life, a steady rock she could rely on.

From the kitchen table inside, Gia's phone buzzed, breaking up her musings. She swung her legs to the floor, intending to step back into the house to retrieve the phone, but Winston stopped her. "I'll get it. Stay put."

"I should get up. I'm starting to get stiff," she said, standing on her feet and taking the last sip of her drink. She rolled her head around.

Winston returned, taking her glass and passing the phone to her. Absently, Gia read the text message and set the phone back on the table, thinking about Dre. He'd looked like a lost little boy when she left, and she'd been close to turning back and insisting he take her to Nashville with him. He shouldn't have been left to deal with seeing his friend alone.

"Everything ok?" Winston asked, pouring her a refill.

"Yeah, Dre just let me know he made it to Nashville," Gia said, then let out a breath. "Maybe I should have gone with him. He seemed like he could use a friend."

She looked up to find Winston studying her intensely. He had something to say, she could tell.

He dropped his gaze. "I don't think you should get so caught up in him, Gia. You don't know that man."

Gia ran a finger along the rim of her glass. If he'd asked, she would have declined another round, opting for a cold glass of water instead. Her head was starting to swim a little. "You said that earlier. I know I don't know him well, but I can tell when someone is hurting. He just found out his best friend might not survive the night. Wouldn't you need a friend if you'd gotten that news about me?"

Sighing, Winston rose from the chair and started pacing.

"Yeah, maybe, but what we want isn't always what we get. I'm sure he's got other friends in Nashville he can lean on." He turned back to her. "You need to keep your distance and concentrate on your recovery, that's all I'm saying."

Now he sounded like her older brother. Why did the men in her life all assume they knew what was best for her?

"I sense there's something more going on here than you're letting on. What's your issue with Dre?" Gia said, crossing her arms and waiting.

"Hell, for starters, I don't buy that he just happened to move here after you two met. That seems too coincidental for my taste, but maybe it's just me." Winston took another pull from his drink. "Why would he move to this small town, Gia? This isn't a place for young, single men; this is where you settle down and raise a family."

"So, what do you think his angle is? What does he want, since you seem to have all these answers?" Gia leaned back in her chair, waiting. "Clearly you have him all figured out, don't you?"

Winston sat down. "I think he's targeting you. Andreas Delaney has a history of dating older women and stealing from them."

CHAPTER 9

Dre

D re stared numbly at his phone, his mind struggling to process the news he'd just received. He had just checked into a hotel near the hospital and his best friend, Darius, the one who'd convinced him to move to Nashville, his running buddy, was gone. Dre hadn't gotten to say goodbye.

The family assured him that they'd call with funeral arrangements but right now, there wasn't anything he could do. Dre stared around at the beige walls of the hotel room. Nashville didn't feel like home. Maybe he hadn't lived there long enough, but he felt something was missing from the city now that Darius was gone.

Without thinking about it, Dre threw his duffle bag in the back, got in his car, and hit the road. He eventually ended up at his mother's lake cabin outside Nashville. It was a place he hadn't been to in years, but he knew he needed to escape the memories of Nashville and be alone with his thoughts. When he arrived, he found the cabin just as he remembered it – secluded, cozy, and surrounded by trees. There were no neighbors nearby, and the only sounds were those of nature: the hoot of an owl responding to songbirds.

He opened the door and stepped inside, feeling almost like he had come home again. His mother, true to form, liked to redecorate her spaces every few years and this place had gotten an upgrade since he'd last spent time here. The whole space was done in his mother's signature French Country style: lots of wood elements balanced with furniture made to look older than it was and glitzy, feminine pieces scattered throughout.

Taking a seat on a tufted couch that looked as if it had just been delivered, Dre closed his eyes for a moment, letting all of these memories wash over him like waves at sea. His grandmother would bring him here during the summer and they'd enjoy the quiet while waiting for his mother to wrap up another show or shoot. She'd tell them to meet her here then they spent half the time waiting for her arrival.

Dre hadn't minded. He spent quality time with his grandmother in this house where they'd bake bread and he experienced the lake under open Tennessee air. He knew that coming here wasn't going to bring his friend back, but there was comfort simply being in this place that used to bring him so much joy growing up.

The first few days in the cabin, Dre was in a daze, his mind constantly replaying memories of his friend. He didn't eat, slept fitfully when his body forced him to rest, and barely left the cabin. He was lost, unsure what to do with himself.

Thoughts of Gia were never far away. He bounced between concern that she was taking her medications on schedule and jealousy that she was staying with another man to wanting to hear her voice.

But he didn't call her.

Tired of wallowing in sorrow, Dre got up early one morning and decided he needed to explore, get out of his own head and be in nature for a while. Dre grabbed some water bottles and snacks before heading off on a hike on the main road near the lake.

Starting off at a brisk pace, Dre focused on his breathing. The morning air was cool and damp but as he walked, the breeze hitting his skin felt good. Veering off onto a wooded path that led to public access to the lake, Dre stopped to watch the water as it flowed in gentle waves toward him. Watching the water calmed him and he sat down on a large rock, taking in his surroundings. He had the lake to himself save a lone fishing boat a few miles away.

As he sat there in silence, his mind raced but he became clear on what he needed to do.

Standing up, he continued his hike, using the fresh air and solitude to work through his plan. While he hadn't been able to save his friend, he could put their plan into motion.

When Dre returned to the cabin, he turned his phone on. He'd kept it off for most of his time at the cabin, he'd needed to shut the world out.

Dre scrolled through the missed calls and messages as his stomach growled. He hadn't had much of an appetite since he'd arrived and now as he perused the pantry, he realized there was no food in the house.

He was placing an order through a delivery service app when his phone rang.

Dre finished his order then peered at the phone's display. Seeing it was Gia, he hesitated for a moment before answering, unsure if he was ready to talk to anyone, including her, about his friend.

"Hey," he said, his voice hoarse.

"Dre, I've been calling...I'm so sorry," Gia replied, concern evident in her voice. "I heard about your friend. How are you feeling?"

He started to say he was ok, but that wasn't true. Dre felt a lump form in his throat, and he swallowed hard before speaking. "I've been better," he said, then added, "I needed to get away."

"Where are you? When I called, the guys at Derby Nights said you'd resigned, but they hadn't heard from you."

Dre hung his head. He hadn't told anyone where he was going. "My mother has a cabin near Old Hickory Lake."

"Wait...I know where that is...Skye hosted a girls getaway weekend there." There was silence for a beat then Gia spoke. "Dre, I'm coming to the cabin," she said firmly. "You shouldn't be alone right now."

Dre's heart skipped a beat at the thought of seeing Gia again. They hadn't really spoken since he'd told her she needed to stay with Winston and he wasn't allowing himself to think about what that meant.

Dre knew that when he'd come home earlier than usual the night he found out about his best friend that Winston was trying to convince Gia he was no good.

"Okay," he said before he could talk himself out of it. "Thank you, Gia."

Dre hung up the phone, feeling a mix of relief and apprehension. He didn't know what to expect from Gia's visit, but he knew he didn't want to be alone anymore. He spent the rest of the day cleaning up the cabin, making it presentable for his unexpected guest.

The sunset was just starting to spread its golden hues over the lake when Dre heard the sound of a car pulling up. He went outside and saw Gia's car, her silhouette visible behind the windshield. He walked towards her car as she stepped out, looking stunning in a simple sundress that hugged her curves. With her curly hair pulled up in a high ponytail and little makeup, she reminded him of a carefree teen.

"Dre," she said, wrapping her arms around him in a tight embrace. "I'm so sorry for your loss."

Dre felt his emotions swell within him, but he managed to hold them back. He looked down at Gia, her eyes filled with compassion and understanding. Without saying a word, he pulled her close and held her tightly. In that moment, he held a glimmer of hope that things might be ok.

Gia searched his face, her hand reaching up to cup his cheek.

Dre closed his eyes, savoring the warmth of her touch. It had been so long since he had been this close to her. Her scent, a soft floral that made him think of sunshine and springtime, filled his senses, and he felt his heart rate increase. He was playing a dangerous game having her here, looking at him like she might feel the same as he did.

Gia pulled back slightly, looking up at Dre with concern. "Are you okay?" she asked softly.

Dre opened his eyes, his gaze locking with hers. "I will be," he said, his voice low and unsteady. "I'm glad you're here."

Gia nodded silently and wrapped her arms around him again in a comforting hug. They stayed like this for a few moments as the sun slowly set over the lake behind them. Finally, Gia pulled away but kept hold of one of his hands as she said quietly, "Come on...let's go inside."

He watched her, standing there, her small hand grasping his. She'd dropped everything to be at his side. He'd feared leaving her in Winston's care might have been the biggest mistake of his life; Winston wanted Gia for himself and if he was in the other man's shoes, he'd do everything in his power to convince Gia that she belonged with him. But Winston had known her for a long time and he hadn't closed the deal. And now she was here, with him and they were alone in a cabin, their own little world, free from his mother, her brother, Winston and all the other normal distractions.

Once they were inside, she sat on the couch, her legs folded under her, and patted the seat beside her. "Tell me about your friend?"

He told her about his friend, relived the funny stories and the not so funny moments where he'd cautioned his friend against his choices. She listened, holding his hand, or rubbing his shoulder, giving him a moment when he needed it.

They sat on the couch talking until well past dark, sharing a bottle of wine and a bag of pretzels Dre had ordered on impulse.

At one point, Gia stood up from the sofa and stretched her legs. "I want to hear about the idea you both had for creating a performing arts school. Should we open another bottle of wine or do you want something stronger?" She looked expectantly at him, her eyes bright.

In that moment, Dre realized that he was falling for Gia. Maybe he had been since he laid eyes on her at the club in Nashville. She had dropped everything, no questions asked and come to him when he was at his lowest point.

He rose and approached her. Taking her face in his hands, he kissed her, slowly, conveying the love for her that he couldn't utter with words.

Gia's lips, one of his favorite parts of her body, were soft, warm, and willing. Dre felt a wave of desire wash over him. He deepened the kiss, his hands moving down to her waist as he pulled her closer. Gia responded eagerly, her fingers tangling in his hair as she kissed him back.

For a long while, they stayed locked in that embrace.

Dre couldn't believe how much he wanted her, how much he needed her. "I'm glad you're here."

Gia nodded, "I had to come and see about you." She caressed the back of his neck, bringing him down for another intense kiss that threatened to buckle his knees.

When they finally broke apart, gasping for breath, Dre looked at Gia with a mix of fear and longing.

This was more than a fling for him now. He'd missed having her in his space and now that she was here, he couldn't stop touching her. He wanted to sink himself into her but she was still recovering.

And suddenly a thought occurred to him.

"Your week is up, isn't it?" he said, referring to her doctor's orders of no strenuous activity while she recovered.

Gia's eyes darkened and she nodded slowly. "All clear."

Dre gave her a slow grin. "Good to know."

"And why is that? You got plans for me?" She raised a brow at him and his blood heated.

"Yep. My mission tonight is to see how many times I can watch you come." He pulled her flush with his body. He felt her hardened nipples against his chest and realized she wasn't wearing a bra. He slid an eager hand up her thigh, under the gauzy dress, past her waist and over her back.

"No bra? Were you hoping to get lucky tonight, love?" he said, sliding his hands back down her back, past her hips. Gripping her cheeks, he lifted her up to give him access to the braless nipples. Gia locked her legs around his waist and Dre could feel her heat through her panties. Why he didn't take them off before he'd hoisted her up, he didn't know.

He walked her to the wall next to the refrigerator. Dre pressed her there, dry humping her as he pinned her hands above her head.

He bent, taking one of the taut peaks in his mouth, sucking it through the dress material.

"No, well, maybe," Gia's head dropped back against the wall, "too hot for a bra...can't really think when you're doing that," she said breathlessly.

"Good. What else do you want me to do, Gia?" He switched nipples as she arched in response.

"Never been smashed against the wall...I like this..." She breathed, nipping his shoulder with her teeth.

"I didn't plan this well..." he ground out, "clothes off first then wall."

"Hang on," Gia reached back, crossing her arms and pulling her dress over her head. She tugged his t-shirt off with one arm while pressing the other arm to the wall to help support herself.

Dre had to admit this woman, *his woman*, was a master at thinking on her feet.

She thrust her hips, rubbing her crotch against his erection and he almost lost it.

He felt her hands roam down his abs, stopping to unbutton his jeans. *Yes.*

Gia tugged at the next button. "Oh my God...you pick today for button fly cargo shorts?"

"Like I said, poor planning on my part," he muttered into her neck. "When I put these on earlier, I had no idea you'd be here, much less trying to rip them off me, but let's try this..." He glanced over at the island.

He carried Gia over to the island and plopped her down. Dre hooked a thumb under her black panties, sliding them down and off. He knew his mother would kill him if she knew he was using her kitchen as his personal sex den, but he couldn't care about that right now.

She leaned back on her elbows, fully nude with her knees open, looking like the best gift ever. He kissed her knee, then licked his way down her thighs. He could smell her heat. He could feel her anticipation as her breath came in quick bursts. He stuck his tongue out, ready to taste her.

As soon as the tip of his tongue met her warm, wet flesh, Gia jerked, pushing her hips forward. "Yes..." she ran her hands through his hair as he probed her with his mouth.

Gia screamed his name, her body jerking as her orgasm ripped through her.

Dre raised his head, satisfied with himself. Grabbing a paper towel from a nearby dispenser, he wiped his mouth and returned to his position between Gia's legs. He gave her a deep kiss. "So. Since you're the guest, where do you want me next?"

Gia blinked like he'd spoken a foreign language then smirked at him. "You lay me out in your mother's kitchen and now you want to know where I want you? Inside me is always gonna be the answer," she said finally. "But drop those," she motioned at his shorts, "and put me back on the wall. Please."

"Yes ma'am." Dre lost his shorts and boxer briefs. Taking a condom from the wallet he'd tossed on the kitchen counter and after putting it on, he picked Gia up, kissed her again and pressed her back against the wall. Again she wrapped her legs around his waist but this time, he slid inside her wetness. Her muscles clenched him tightly and he almost lost it.

"Oh..." Gia threw her head back and closed her eyes, hoisting her hips and giving him deeper access. Dre pumped harder as Gia shuddered and moaned, squeezing him even tighter as she came.

Dre kept going, giving her one final deep thrust before calling her name and exploding.

"Dre." Gia's voice was husky, sexy. She wiped tears from her eyes with one hand and stroked his sweaty chest with the other. "You," she said, panting hard, "are amazing."

CHAPTER 10
Winston

Winston sighed as he strode into the space that would eventually become Lush Lingerie. That morning, he'd gotten up early for a workout at J&J Fitness, picked up a cup of coffee from French Kiss, and now he was ready to start his workday.

He greeted the construction crew, then slipped past them to the back storage area where his desk was. He had been using the back as a makeshift office for the past few weeks, and he was happy to see that nothing had been disturbed in his absence. He liked to have his desk organized just so and as he evaluated the items, he noted with satisfaction that everything was neatly arranged and in its place.

The store renovation was progressing, despite Gia's absence as she recovered from surgery. He glanced at the calendar on his laptop. Technically, her recovery week was up but she was still in Tennessee with Dre, doing God knows what. He sighed, thinking of the last time they'd said more than a handful of words to each other.

He'd attempted to explain what he'd found out, what he'd read about Dre, who had been involved with a woman in her forties who accused him of stealing her credit cards to pay his bills.

But she'd cut him off.

Winston sighed as he remembered Gia's words before she'd run off to be with Dre.

"Win, I don't have anything for Dre to steal. He saved my life, and I don't think he would have done that if he wanted to steal my money. He's had multiple opportunities to take my credit cards, maxed out as they are."

"Gia, I'm just saying that Dre is not the kind of guy you should be hanging out with. He's bad news," Winston said, his voice tinged with frustration.

Gia rolled her eyes. "Winston, you don't know anything about him. He's been nothing but good to me."

Winston let out a sarcastic laugh. "Really? Are you making decisions with your mind or are you letting your other body parts decide?" He knew as soon as the words left his mouth that he'd gone too far but he couldn't help himself.

Gia shook her head. "That's not any of your concern, first of all, but to answer your question, I do one hundred percent of my thinking with my brain," she tapped the side of her head in emphasis. "You might have done better to use yours when you were dealing with your ex, since apparently we're going there with judgment."

Winston clenched his fists. "So, what exactly are you saying?"

"I'm saying, I don't believe you used your best judgement with your ex. I think you got caught up in her looks."

He couldn't believe Gia had turned the tables on him. "Well, maybe I did but it's done now. I'm trying to make you see reason so that you don't get your heart broken."

Why couldn't she see Dre's true nature? "Gia, please listen to me. I care about you and I'm worried."

Gia's expression hardened. "Winston, I appreciate your concern, but I know what I'm doing. When I need your advice, I will seek it. I'm going to bed."

He knew she was stubborn, but he couldn't believe that Gia had chosen to side with Dre, a man she barely knew, over him.

And now she was in a cabin with him while Winston fought to get her business going. He slammed a fist on the table in frustration, angry that she had chosen to prioritize Dre over their business and their friendship.

He sat down at his desk and tried to focus on his work, but his mind kept drifting back to Gia and Dre.

He took a deep breath and tried to shake off the anger. He had work to do and Lush Lingerie wasn't going to build itself. He began to go over the plans and timeline for the store, making sure every detail was perfect. As he worked, he couldn't help but think about Gia and Dre together. Did she even care about him anymore? Did she miss him at all? Winston tried to push those thoughts away, but they kept creeping back into his mind.

As the day wound to a close, Winston heard the construction crew packing up and soon, the store was quiet, leaving him alone with his thoughts. This was ridiculous, he thought as he picked up the phone to call Gia. They needed to get over this rift between them and move on.

Phone in hand, he looked up as he heard the front door creak open. Assuming one of the workers had forgotten something, he didn't immediately get up and resumed his attempt to call Gia.

A familiar voice rang out. "Hello? Gia? You here?"

Winston ended the call then stood quickly, straightening his desk then smoothing his clothes before he rushed to the front.

"Skye, nice to see you again," he said, rushing over to shake her hand. "I didn't know you were back in town."

"Thank you, Winston. Where is Gia? I sent her a text telling her I would be in Kentucky and she told me that now wasn't a good time to check on the store." Skye looked around, a puzzled look on her face. "I thought there would be more done in here by now."

"We've hit some roadblocks with permits, but it's all been cleared up." Winston tried to hide his disappointment that Gia hadn't mentioned Skye's visit to him. "She's actually out of town right now, but I can give her a call and let her know you stopped by."

Skye crossed her arms. "Out of town? Where did she go?"

Winston hesitated for a moment, unsure if he should reveal Gia's whereabouts. But he figured Skye was Dre's mother and she had a right to know. "She went to see about Dre after she found out his best friend died," he finally admitted.

Skye's eyes widened in surprise. "Who died? And where are they?"

Winston raised an eyebrow. How did he know more about the woman's son than she did? "Dre's best friend in Nashville was in a bad accident...they rushed him to the hospital, but he didn't pull through. Dre went to Nashville to see him when he got the news that his friend was gone."

All of the irritation he'd sensed from Skye was gone. Skye visibly blanched. "Do you know his friend's name? I can't believe Andreas didn't call me."

She dug through her purse, plucking her phone out.

Winston watched as she tried to get Dre on the phone. They both waited, listening to the rings as Dre's phone went unanswered.

The volume on Skye's phone was louder than normal and Winston heard the man's voicemail prompt.

Skye spoke into the phone. "Andreas, this is your mother. Please call me and let me know what's going on and where you are."

She ended the call, then turned fiery green eyes on Winston. "You don't know where they are?"

Winston shrank a bit under her scrutiny. "Not exactly. A cabin somewhere in Tennessee? Near a body of water, a lake maybe, but I can't recall..."

"Old Hickory Lake?"

Snapping his finger, Winston nodded. "Yes, that's it."

"Makes sense. That's my cabin and Andreas used to spend summers there," Skye said.

Her shoulders slumped. "Why wouldn't he tell me? He shouldn't be grieving alone," Skye said more to herself than to Winston.

She looked up at Winston suddenly. "As you can probably tell, my son and I aren't close," she admitted. "I'm not sure what to do. Should I go see about him?"

Her voice was quiet but Winston heard the uncertainty and pain in it.

He paused, unsure how much to tell her. "Gia's there. I haven't really heard from her since she told me she made it but I assume she'd have said something if there was a problem."

"I see." Skye's eyes met Winston's as he fought an urge not to squirm under her steel gaze. He felt like he'd been caught stealing penny candy from the corner store.

She lifted her shoulders. "So, am I correct in assuming there's something going on between my son and Gia?"

"That's a question you would have to ask them," he said slowly.

Skye continued to study him and Winston felt himself fidgeting under her scrutiny. He imagined this is what Dre felt like as a child when he'd done something bad.

"And how are you feeling about these recent developments?" she finally asked.

Winston stared straight ahead. Talk about a loaded question. He thought Gia was making a huge mistake and that her judgment was clouded by a young, firm muscular body, but he wouldn't share that with the man's mother. "Everyone here is an adult and can make their own choices," he said, his voice neutral.

"When you and I met, I got the distinct impression you want more than friendship from her," Skye said, crossing her arms. "I realize you are treading lightly because of my son and because you don't know me but hear me out." Skye walked around the space. "I'm not thrilled to hear about Andreas and my mentee, especially when neither of them bothered to clue me in, so if there's something you would like for me to do or say to intervene on your behalf, please let me know."

She strode back over to his desk then handed him a business card from her purse.

"What do you mean by 'intervene'?" Winston asked, taking the card. "I don't want any involvement in anything that might hurt her."

"Oh my, you are in deep, aren't you, Winston? I know my son is captivating to a lot of women, but he's young, especially for Gia, and I imagine he won't stick around long. She needs a man who will be ok with being in the background once she achieves success. You seem to fit that bill. You think you can get her to move back to New York?"

Winston had enough. "You know your son's a stripper, right? Gia met him in Nashville during one of his shows and now he's joined the Santa Revue here in Kissing Springs."

Skye's eyes narrowed. "I'm headed to my cabin to see about my son."

On the surface, Winston noted that Skye hid her shock well. He could tell she was pissed, and he sent up a little prayer that he wasn't the source of it.

With that, she turned and strode out of the store.

Winston let out a long breath as the door closed behind her. He rubbed his temples, feeling a headache coming on. The last thing he needed was for Skye to get involved in his personal life. But a small part of him was grateful for the offer. He still cared about Gia and he didn't want to lose her to Dre.

He picked up Skye's card and studied it for a moment. He wondered if he should call her and tell her about his concerns. But he quickly dismissed the idea. He didn't want to cause any drama or make things worse.

He put the card back on his desk. A little voice inside urged him to let Gia know that Dre's mother was on her way, but he decided to let the drama unfold as it was meant to. Gia might need a shoulder to cry on after the dust settled.

She was in over her head with Dre and the sooner she figured that out, the better.

CHAPTER 11

Dre

D re and Gia lay on the queen-sized bed in the room that was once his. He held her close, his arms wrapped protectively around her. He wanted to keep them in this bubble forever, away from all of their troubles.

Gia stirred slightly and Dre wondered if she was awake. He decided to take the chance and softly whispered, "Did you miss me, Gia?" He hated to ask but needed to know.

Gia responded immediately and tenderly, her hand caressing Dre's. "I'm here. I dropped everything because I knew you'd need a friend." Her words were like a balm to Dre's soul, filling him with a warmth and peace he hadn't felt in a long time. He was so grateful that Gia had come and was here with him now.

"This is more than friendship for me, Gia," he said, his heart racing. Dre hadn't intended to bare everything but now that the words were free, he couldn't call them back.

She shifted to face him, her eyes roaming his face. "What are you saying?"

"I'm saying I want more. I've been driving myself crazy thinking I sent you straight to Winston when all I wanted was for you to be mine."

Gia rose up resting her head on her fist. "Dre, I won't deny I have feelings for you but this isn't the right time for us. You're mourning and I'm trying to get a business off the ground. I have poured everything I have into this business, and it has to work, there's no plan B." She stroked his cheek. "And I'm not sure a serious relationship with an older woman who's a workaholic is really what you want at this stage in your life. You should be out having fun."

He looked away, feeling the sting of her words. "I'm where I want to be."

Dre knew she had a point. He was mourning, and he wasn't sure if he was ready for a serious relationship either. But he couldn't deny the way he felt about her. He wanted her, and not just for a fling as she'd suggested before.

"I can't help how I feel about you, Gia. And I don't think I can just turn it off."

Gia reached out, rubbing his arm. "I know, Dre. And I'm not saying I don't feel the same way about you. It's just that right now, it's not the right time for us."

Dre sighed. That was not what he wanted to hear but he guessed it was better than nothing. "I get that. So now what? You running back to Winston?"

She shook her head. "No. You know I'm not."

Dre nodded and scooted back toward the edge of the bed, putting a few inches of space between them. He wanted to keep her close but knew she was right; it wasn't the right time for them.

Gia looked up at him with sad eyes. "I'm sorry, Dre. We have to end this before we're both in too deep and hearts get broken."

As he watched her move away from him, a heavy weight settled in his chest.

Too late.

"Why are you doing this, Gia?" Dre asked, his voice low and dangerous.

"Doing what?" Gia replied, turning toward him as she gathered her discarded clothing.

"Pushing me away. Acting like you don't want to be with me."

Gia sighed. "It's not that I don't have feelings for you, Dre. I think you're a great man, but I don't feel like you know what you want and that includes me. I don't think you'll be happy staying at home while I put in the hours needed to get my store off the ground. Then you'll find some young woman, probably at one of your shows, who is willing to ease your pain and next thing I know, you're cheating on me."

Dre shook his head, feeling a little hurt at her low opinion of him. "That's not fair, Gia. You don't know me well enough to make that kind of judgement. I take relationships seriously and if I decide to be with someone, I will be loyal and honest with them."

Gia nodded slowly and reached out to stroke his cheek again. "I know that, Dre. And I wish things could be different, but it just isn't the right time for us."

Dre grabbed her hand in his and held it tightly, refusing to let go despite how badly he wanted to pull her into an embrace. He couldn't deny what he was feeling anymore; he wanted this woman in his life, and he was determined to prove to her that she didn't have anything to worry about with him.

"Give me a chance, Gia," he pleaded softly, looking deep into her eyes so she could see the sincerity in his. "Let me prove that I'm the man you need." He paused for a moment before adding "I can give you all of myself - physically, emotionally and spiritually."

Finally, Gia shook her head. "I can't do this, Dre. Not now. I need to leave and figure out what I want and if you're a part of that. It's just too complicated with our lives going in different directions. So please understand, this is goodbye...we both need a break."

"Fine," he said, turning away from her. "Take your space. But don't expect me to wait around forever."

Dre walked out of the room, unable to watch Gia pack her things.

Grabbing a bottle of water from the refrigerator, he stomped out to the back deck and slumped into one of the chairs.

Gia walked out, carrying the duffle bag he'd loaned her.

She looked like she had been crying.

At least he wasn't the only miserable one.

"I need to get into your apartment to get my suitcase," she said, avoiding his eyes.

He turned toward the lake. "There's a spare key on my key chain in the kitchen. It's a light blue key," he sighed. "I actually had that key made for you so you can toss it when you're done."

His voice almost broke and he took a pull of his water.

Gia exhaled before speaking. "Dre, I know this sounds cliché but I never intended to hurt you. God, I hate when people say that," she took a step toward him, "but I mean it. When I met you, watched you dance, I couldn't take my eyes off you. I was mesmerized, then when you brought me on stage, I was so attracted to you, but I figured it was part of the show, you know, what you guys do to make as much in tips as you can."

She looked away. "After the show, you seemed so interested in me, again, I assumed it was all part of the illusion and I invited you up to my room, figuring, Hey, I'll indulge this one fantasy before I have to go back to my old bedroom at my parents' house. I'll never see this man again, but we both know how that turned out."

Gia stopped, taking a deep breath.

"Why did you think I wouldn't be interested in you? You're a beautiful woman," Dre broke in.

"I mean, I'm not saying I'm chopped liver or anything, but guys like you don't typically go for the geeky girls like me. I didn't think it was real, your interest. Then Winston told me you have a thing for older women." She shrugged.

He sighed. He knew eventually that she'd find out about that incident. "I never stole anything from anyone. Yes, I was dating an older woman. She was married and rather than admit to her affair and her willingness to spend her husband's money on me, she accused me of stealing from her." He looked Gia in the eye then. "I was young and stupid and learned my lesson. No more married women."

Exhaling, she nodded in confirmation. "I never thought you were into me to steal from me but there is this little voice inside… it's hard for me to trust these days," she said.

Dre watched as Gia spoke, feeling a pang of regret for lashing out at her earlier. He had been hurt by her rejection, but he could see now that she had her own fears and doubts.

"I get it." Dre took another swig from his water and turned to look at her. "I just wish things were different."

Gia walked closer to him, her hand reaching out to touch his shoulder. "Me too," she whispered.

They stood there for a moment, holding each other's gaze before Gia finally pulled away, picking up the duffle bag. "I should go."

Dre nodded, watching her walk out of the cabin.

* * *

Dre halfheartedly folded his clothes, lost in thought as he replayed the events of his breakup with Gia over and over in his mind. He couldn't shake the ache in his chest, pain made worse because he could no longer call his best friend to talk about it.

The cabin held too many memories now and he was ready to head back to Kissing Springs. He'd deal with those memories later.

As he folded one of the t-shirts Gia had borrowed from him, lost in his sadness, he was jarred out of his thoughts by the sound of a car pulling up outside. He glanced out the window, a small part of him hoping it was Gia coming back to say she changed her mind.

He watched with dread as his mother stepped out of her car.

Dre's heart sank as he saw his mother approach the house. He wasn't mentally prepared for a visit from her, especially not now with his emotions still raw from his breakup with Gia.

He quickly tried to compose himself before his mother walked in, taking deep breaths to calm his racing heart. But as soon as she stepped inside, he knew it was pointless. His mother had always had a way of seeing right through him.

"What are you doing here?" Dre asked, shocked to see Skye. He hadn't spoken to her since she'd come to Kissing Springs.

"I had to come check on you," Skye said, pushing past him and into the cabin. "I've been trying to call you, but you haven't been answering."

Dre sighed, closing the door behind her. He didn't want to deal with his mother right now, not when he was still trying to process his breakup and his grief. "I'm fine, I just needed some time alone."

"Andreas...I don't even know where to start. Why am I having to hear about your life from other people? I didn't know you and Gia knew each other and now you're...dating?" she said, crossing her arms.

"Nope," he said, shaking his head. "It's over. So, you can save whatever speech you had planned. She's gone."

"Andreas, I don't think you and Gia..."

Dre waited for her to continue but she studied him without a word.

Finally, she spoke. "You love her, don't you?"

He nodded, then went back to gathering his things.

"I take it the break up wasn't your idea?"

Hell no.

He didn't answer.

"Are you leaving?" Skye asked. "I just got here...I was thinking maybe we could have some wine and talk."

The last thing Dre wanted to do was rehash their long-standing arguments right then, but he'd never been able to deny his mother anything.

He stood there, taking her in. His mother, as usual, was dressed for a fashion shoot with all of her hair in place, full makeup on, and a designer outfit. It was like she'd walked onto stage, in full concerned mother mode after studying her lines in her trailer.

But if he didn't know better, he'd swear his mother looked hopeful, which wasn't an emotion he normally expected of Skye Delaney.

He shrugged. "I was heading back to Kissing Springs. I need to try to figure out what I want to do now that I don't have a job."

"You quit the strip club already?"

She patted his arm. "Son, come on, let's break open one of those expensive wines I have in the chiller. I can tell you about my last heartbreak." She paused, throwing a coy glance. "And I have edibles if you're game."

Dre's eyebrows rose in shock. His mother, the driven no-nonsense, just-say-no mother was offering him drugs? Who was this woman? "Umm...let's stick to the wine. I'm not sure I'm ready to experience my mother high as a 747."

Skye chuckled, leading the way to the kitchen where she retrieved a bottle of red wine and two glasses. Dre watched as she expertly uncorked the bottle and poured them both a generous amount.

As they sat down at the small table, Skye took a sip of her wine before turning to Dre with a serious expression. "So, tell me what's been going on in your life."

Dre sighed, swirling his glass of wine as he recounted the death of his best friend and his breakup with Gia. Skye listened intently, asking questions, and nodding sympathetically when he finished. When he was done, she refilled their glasses before speaking.

"I's sorry to hear about your friend Darius. I wish I'd gotten to meet him. As for Gia, I think the breakup is for the best," she peered at him closely, "you need to think about what happens when she's successful. You think having a young stripper on her arm will be an asset or a liability? It's different for women, son."

Skye reached across the table and squeezed his hand reassuringly. "Listen Andreas, I know it hurts but sometimes breakups are necessary - even if it doesn't feel like it right now."

He nodded slowly, processing her words before responding quietly, "I just don't know what to do now."

"Well," Skye said thoughtfully, taking another sip of wine before continuing. "You'll figure it out, but in the meantime why don't you come work for me? I'm funding startups and I could use your help."

He sighed. This was her default. Trying to fix things she assumed were broken by throwing money at them. "I don't see myself sitting behind a desk all day pushing papers around."

"You wouldn't be pushing papers. I'm trying to elevate women and minority owned businesses by providing guidance and funding. You would be making a real change in the world.

"So, what are you saying, Mother?" He clenched his jaw.

"I'm saying you can't have it both ways. If you're going to continue stripping," she rested a hand on her chin. "Let her go."

"I don't think it's fair to ask me to choose between my job and my relationship," he said, trying to keep his voice steady. "And honestly, I don't think Gia cares about what I do for a living. She accepts me for who I am, not what I do."

Snorting, Skye continued. "She may not care, but the world will judge her; the industry won't take her seriously, and her career will suffer. And that will take its toll on your relationship. Trust me on this."

Dre stood up, pacing around the kitchen. His mother's words hit a nerve. He didn't want to admit it, but part of him knew she was right. The world was judgmental, especially when it came to women and their partners. Maybe their breakup was for the best.

CHAPTER 12

Gia

On a dark Saturday morning in November, Gia stood in the middle of Lush Lingerie, taking in all the tiny details she tended to stress over.

Lush Lingerie was a quaint little store, tucked away in the corner of Main Street, surrounded by various mom-and-pop shops that gave the area a small-town charm. But, once you step inside, the shop is transformed into a modern, upscale lingerie paradise.

The walls were a soft pink hue, adorned with framed photos of women of all shapes, sizes, and colors confidently wearing different styles of lingerie. The store was well-lit, yet cozy, with tall shelves displaying neatly folded bras, panties, and stockings. The scents of lavender and vanilla filled the air, adding to the serene ambiance.

She glanced at the time on her watch. She had about three hours to go before her soft open at ten a.m. The 3D printers were ready to go. They would be running quick demos of making fabric samples using the printer so visitors could see and touch the material.

The models were due in at eight and she needed to make sure they had everything they needed. They would be doing mini fashion shows on a red carpet in the front of the store then circulating through the interior.

As she prepared to open the doors of Lush for the first time, she had a secret wish that Dre would be one of her models. She had designed a look especially for him and sent it to his apartment with an invitation asking if he'd model. The silence weighed on her like a heavy stone- there was no response. It had been months since they last spoke, since the summer when everything fell apart.

Gia stopped for a moment to think about Dre. She'd been so busy getting the store ready that she hadn't had time to reflect on them, or so she told herself, but in moments like this one, she admitted that she missed him.

And that fear was stopping her from giving in to her heart's desire.

She shook her head, trying to clear her thoughts. "Get it together, Gia," she whispered to herself, taking a deep breath. She couldn't let her personal life affect her professional life, especially not today.

After leaving Skye's cabin and Dre behind, Gia had returned to Kissing Springs, collected her things from Dre's, then gone to Winston's and done the same.

Winston had confessed that he told Skye about them and that Dre was working as a stripper. Gia had been furious but in hindsight, maybe it was best that Skye knew the truth.

She turned her attention back to the store, making sure everything was perfect for the soft open. Gia had put her heart and soul into this business, and she was determined to make it a success. She had a vision for Lush Lingerie, and nothing was going to stop her from achieving it.

As she was hanging up a new, lacy bralette, the doorbell chimed. Gia looked up to see her niece, Jordyn Mitchell, walk in, carrying two large cups of coffee and a huge tote bag.

"Hey Auntie! I got us coffee! We ready to do this thing?" Jordyn set down two large cups of coffee and a huge tote bag on the counter where customers would pay for their purchases.

Gia grabbed her niece in a big hug, happy to see her. "Jordyn, I am so glad you're here! And bonus points for the coffee."

Thankful for the distraction, Gia smiled at her niece, taking in her appearance. Jordyn was petite and looked exactly like Jameson, Gia's older brother. She had his walnut-colored skin and deep brown expressive eyes. Jordyn, beaming at her, had her big curly hair pulled up into a high ponytail, and she wore a pair of oversized, round glasses. She was dressed in a trendy, yet comfortable outfit, with a cropped sweater, high-waisted jeans, and a pair of white sneakers.

Gia fluffed Jordyn's hair out. "You look cute, you sure you don't want to model today?"

Jordyn handed Gia a coffee, then pulled her iPad from her tote bag. "Nope. I'll leave that to the professionals. All right, so we have the models coming in at eight, and the mini fashion shows start at ten. We have a lot to do before then."

Gia nodded, impressed by Jordyn's organizational skills. "You're amazing, Jordyn. Thank you for all your help."

Jordyn grinned. "Of course, Auntie. I'm excited to see your store in action. Plus, I'm learning a lot about event planning and marketing."

Gia smiled at her niece's eagerness to learn. "It's a win-win situation for both of us then. Okay," she clapped her hands together, "let's get to work!"

Gia and Jordyn worked together to make sure the store was ready. They tidied up displays, refolded merchandise, and made sure everything looked perfect. Gia hung a few extra pieces of lingerie on mannequins throughout the store and placed mirrors strategically so customers could check out their look from all angles. Jordyn set up her laptop at the front counter for customer purchases and arranged a space for customers to try on garments in the back corner of the store.

As they were setting up, Gia glanced up to see her parents and Jameson approaching the door.

Jameson gave his daughter a half hug as her hands were full of hangers. "Hey Jelly Bean…store looks good, G! And I'm impressed you got this one out of bed so early."

Jordyn rolled her eyes, placing the hangers in a pile near the counter.

"She volunteered to come in early today," Gia said, passing a pile of boy shorts to Jordyn." She's been a godsend."

Gia's mother surveyed the store. "It looks like it's going to be a success, Gia. We're so proud of you."

"Thanks, Mom. I couldn't have done it without your help. Once Skye pulled her investment, I wasn't sure I'd be able to move forward."

Her parents had used a home equity loan to give Gia the additional funding she needed.

"Well, I understand a mother looking out for her child, but I thought it was very unprofessional for Skye to leave you high and dry like that," her mother crossed her arms, "and I deleted all of her shows from my DVR."

Gia chuckled, grateful for her mother's support. "Thank you, Mom."

Finally, just as the first model arrived, Gia surveyed her work with pride. She felt like she had created something beautiful and special, something that would make women feel confident and empowered while they shopped for lingerie. She couldn't wait to show it off today.

Jordyn beamed at Gia's enthusiasm, then gave her a big hug. "You're gonna do great today, Auntie! Let's get this show on the road!"

Just as they were about to finish, Gia heard voices outside the store. She went to the window to see what was going on and noticed a small group of people carrying signs that read ""Keep the robots out of our jobs!" and "Human power only!"

Gia's heart sank as she realized what was happening. It was the old biddies, who didn't want technology taking over their little town, protesting her store before it could even open. She had tried hard not to let it bother her, but seeing them out there made her angry and frustrated.

Gia took a deep breath, trying to steady herself. She knew that she couldn't let these protesters get to her, not now, not ever. She had worked too hard to let them get in the way of her dreams.

Jordyn noticed her expression and walked over to her. "What's going on?"

Gia gritted her teeth, her eyes fixed on the protesters outside. "It's the old biddies."

Jordyn looked outside and then back at Gia. "What do you want to do?"

Gia thought for a moment, then made up her mind. "I'm not going to let them stop me. Let's open the doors."

Jordyn nodded. "Okay, let's do this."

Gia took a deep breath, then walked to the door and unlocked it. The protesters outside noticed her, and their shouts grew louder. "Shut it down! Shut it down!"

Gia ignored them, then turned to Jordyn. "Let's get to work."

Jordyn smiled, then walked over to the counter and began setting up her laptop. Gia walked to the back of the store to greet the models, who were already changing into their lingerie.

Gia took a deep breath and began introducing herself, determined to make this soft opening a success despite the protesters. She smiled warmly at each model as she greeted them, grateful for their support.

The protestors, however, were relentless. They continued to harass people trying to enter the store and even attempted to physically block customers from entering.

Gia felt her frustration rising as they made it increasingly difficult to have a successful soft opening.

At one point, Gia noticed an older woman trying to come into the store while being harassed by two of the protesters. The woman was clearly shaken up and looked like she was about to cry. Without thinking, Gia stepped in between them and attempted to usher the woman inside before locking eyes with the protesters. The woman, shaking her head, turned, and retreated to her car. Gia's heart sank.

"That's enough!" she snapped, her voice firm. "You all have known my family for years and I can't believe you are threatened by one woman opening a lingerie store that helps women feel beautiful. I'm not taking jobs away; I'm actually creating them. My garments are made right here in Kissing Springs, not China."

The protesters looked surprised, but Gia could see that they were listening. She decided to take a chance and stepped closer to them. "I'm sure you have your own worries and concerns," she said, her voice gentle now. "Why don't we talk about them?"

The protesters glanced at each other before one of them nodded slowly. They stepped away from the door and began talking with Gia more calmly while Jordyn kept watch over the store entrance.

Gia leaned against the wall and surveyed the protesters with a tight-lipped expression. Finally, she proclaimed, "All right, I'm willing to come to an agreement. You can keep protesting here as long as it doesn't get in the way of customers entering the store – no harassing or blocking them from getting what they need. But, if you want me to open up my ears and really listen to your grievances about technology taking over our town, then I'll have to find some time in my busy day to sit down with you one-on-one." A protester stepped forward, her voice firm but respectful. "We'd really appreciate that," she said. Gia nodded. "Then it's settled."

Later, after the store was closed and Gia was alone, she sat down on one of the chairs in the fitting room and let the disappointment flow over her. Hot tears full of frustration ran down her cheeks.

She felt like a failure. Sure, she had managed to handle the protesters and keep the soft opening going, but it wasn't the grand success she had envisioned. Winston wasn't there to help her, Dre was gone, and even though Jordyn and her family had pitched in to help out, Gia still felt like she was alone in this.

She wiped away her tears, took a deep breath, and closed her eyes. She knew she couldn't give up. She had worked too hard and sacrificed too much to let this setback defeat her.

Gia thought back to the day she had told her parents about her dream of opening a lingerie store. They had been skeptical at first, but Gia had convinced them that she could make it work. After the drama and loss of her partner and stake in the company she'd put her time, money, and tears into, she was determined to succeed, to prove she could stand on her own.

And she wasn't going to let a few protesters and a disappointing soft opening stop her. Gia was determined to make this store a success; she'd just have to figure something else out.

She'd find a way.

She stood up, brushed off her pants, and walked out of the fitting room. As she surveyed the store, she felt a renewed sense of purpose. She was going to make this work no matter what it took.

Her phone vibrated in her pocket. Gia pulled it out. Her niece Jordyn had posted a video on social media and tagged her in it.

"Hey peeps! I'm here in the Romance Capital of the South, aka Kissing Springs, KY and my aunt Gia, amazing lingerie designer and best aunt ever, had her soft opening today."

Jordyn turned the camera on herself after panning the outside of the store. "These people don't want to see her open the store because she's using 3D printers and they are afraid this business and others like it are killing jobs, when in fact, she's creating jobs."

In the video, Jordyn did a hand motion and the next scene was from the inside of the store. Jordyn stood with one of the college interns she'd hired to run the machines.

"Check out these machines!" Jordyn exclaimed. "They're amazing and they're creating jobs for people in our community. Aunt Gia is doing something really special here."

The intern smiled and added, "I never thought I'd be working with 3D printers, but I love it. And I'm so grateful for the opportunity."

"This is the future! Support small businesses! Support Lush

Lingerie! Till next time, I'm Jordyn." Gia chuckled as Jordyn threw up a peace sign and the video faded to black.

Gia pressed the phone to her heart, a sense of pride and amazement washing over her at the polished, savvy young woman her niece had become. She hadn't even known Jordyn was recording the scene.

Glancing back at her phone, Gia scrolled through some of the comments on the video. Lots of the posters were offering support and words of encouragement. Gia smiled. She assumed most of the people watching were Jordyn's friends and classmates, but it was nice to see nonetheless.

Maybe the soft opening hadn't been the huge success she'd hoped for, but she was creating jobs and making a difference in her community.

She knew that there would be more obstacles in the future, but Gia was ready to face them head-on. She had a renewed sense of purpose and a new determination to make her store a success.

Gia picked up her phone and started typing a response to Jordyn's post. "Thank you for the shoutout, Jordyn. You're the best niece ever. And to all the protesters out there, I'm willing to listen to your concerns and find a way to work together. But I won't let anyone stop me from pursuing my dreams and making a difference in our community. If you're looking for lingerie that is custom designed for you, no matter your size, stop by Lush Lingerie. We will help you fall in love with your body."

With a smile on her face, Gia hit send and continued to plan for the future of her store.

* * *

Gia straightened a display for what seemed like the tenth time then surveyed the rest of her store. She'd done it. She'd gotten the store open, and it was beautiful. Now she just needed customers.

They would come, she knew. She hoped. She wanted to pay

her parents back so they could continue going on their vacations around the world.

Gia heard a noise and froze. She thought she'd locked the front door when she flipped the "closed" sign on, but she wasn't one hundred percent sure of that. Before she could grab her phone and check, she heard her name.

"Gia."

She closed her eyes. Gia loved the way her name rolled off his lips.

God, she missed him. Every night, before she fell asleep, she wondered if she'd done the right thing letting him go. Was she letting fear get in the way of her happiness?

She turned around to face Dre, who was standing just a few feet away from her, holding a bouquet of red roses.

"Dre, what are you doing here?" she asked, her voice catching in her throat.

"I know you need time, but I couldn't stay away from you any longer," he said, stepping closer to her and handing her the flowers. "These are for you."

Gia took the flowers from him, admiring their beauty and breathing in their sweet fragrance.

"Dre, they're beautiful, but…" she trailed off, not sure what to say. Setting the roses on the counter, she crossed her arms.

He looked around. "The store looks good; you did a great job with it."

"Thanks, now all I need is customers."

He nodded. "They'll come. I've been following the updates on social media."

She smiled ruefully. She hadn't had the heart to post recently. "Then I guess you saw my niece's video."

He nodded. "That's partially why I'm here. I have an idea that I need to work through with Dillon and the guys."

Trying not to sound as breathless as she felt, she asked, "What's your idea?"

Dre shook his head. "Not yet. I don't want to spoil it."

"Ok, you know I'm dying to know what it is but I'll stand down." She stepped a little closer to him. "You said that was partially why you were here?"

"Yeah." He closed the distance between them. "I wanted to see you. Make sure you were ok."

"So, you just came to see how I was doing?" she said, suddenly stepping over to a table to straighten the display of boy shorts. She needed to put space between them. His presence was messing with her emotions. "You could have called."

"I could have. But nothing like being in person."

"So, you've seen me."

"You look good." His low growl had her longing to touch him. "You straightened your hair."

"Thank you...yes," She smoothed her hair self-consciously. "I wanted to change it up a bit."

"I like it." His eyes wandered over her and she resisted the urge to fan herself.

Dre cleared his throat. "So, here's my thing. My mother agreed that I needed to leave you alone and let you run your business. I tried," he raised his hands in surrender, "but I can't seem to do that."

Gia's heart skipped a beat at his words. She had missed him so much, but she also couldn't ignore the facts.

She dropped her arms at her sides. "Nothing has changed, Dre. You're still too young for me. I still don't have time for a relationship."

"I can't do anything about my age but what if I want to help you grow your business? What if I want to fully support you in whatever you want to do because I love you and can't live another moment without you?"

"This won't work," Gia's voice broke. She cleared her throat. "I'm scared you're going to find someone closer to your age who wants what you want."

"You're what I want." He turned her toward him and held her face in his hands.

Gia looked up at him, her eyes filled with uncertainty. "But what about what I want?"

"I want to know what you want," he said softly. "I'm not here to pressure you or make you feel like you have to choose. I just want to be here for you, Gia. To love you and support you in whatever you want to do. If that means being friends, then I'm here for that. If it means being more, then I'm here for that too."

Gia's eyes searched his face, as if trying to find something in his expression. "I...I need time," she finally admitted.

Dre nodded, but Gia could see the defeat in his eyes. "Ok, I'll give you the time you need. Just promise me that you'll think about it, that you'll consider giving us a chance."

She nodded, folding her arms around her. Wondering again if she was doing the right thing letting him go, she watched him walk away.

CHAPTER 13
Winston

Winston settled into the aged leather recliner, his eyes closed, as he immersed himself into the music coming through the sound system. He was journeying back through the Motown era, listening to songs created before his time.

As he drummed his fingers to the beat of "Shop Around" by The Miracles, he thought about his time in Kissing Springs. He'd come to town to help Gia. When she'd presented the idea of relocating from Chicago to the small town he'd loved as a younger man, he'd initially said no but in typical Gia fashion, she'd persuaded him, selling him on a fresh start, at least for a year.

The more he thought about it, the more sense it made. Everything in Chicago reminded him of his ex and the life he no longer had. A change of pace was just what he'd needed, and he'd gotten that.

As for Gia, he'd thought that just maybe this was their time.

A new song started. The tempo was slower and Winston chuckled at the irony. Smoky Robinson singing "You Really Got a Hold On Me" poured out of the speakers. Gia Mitchell had a hold on him for the past twenty years and he hadn't even realized it.

But she hadn't chosen him.

She'd spent the remainder of her recovery week with him as he took care of her. They'd worked on the plans for the boutique and bounced ideas off of each other and the time had been like that in college where they seemed to be fully in sync. And hindsight being what it was, he realized that he had mistaken that close camaraderie for love.

They'd settled into a routine where Winston would head to the store to work for a few hours each morning. He'd come back for lunch with Gia. and then they'd work on logistics and whatever issue arose. They'd have dinner, and most times Gia would continue working on her laptop.

They were good and Winston wanted to tell her that they could continue on like that for the rest of their lives. He could buy the house and that would be their home until she wanted something bigger when they started their family. It was going to be perfect, he just had to set everything in motion by professing his love.

While he was working up the courage to put his heart out there, Dre's friend died. As soon as Gia learned that Dre lost his friend, her focus shifted.

They were preparing to go into the store to choose some garment fixtures when Gia stepped out of the kitchen, her phone in hand. "Oh no," she said, putting a hand to her mouth. "Dre's friend didn't make it."

"What? You talked to him?" Winston asked as he slathered avocado on a slice of toast. As far as he knew, Gia hadn't talked to Dre since she'd left his apartment.

"Not yet," she murmured, staring at the phone. "I'm seeing it on social media."

Setting the phone down, Gia looked at him. "Should I call him? Text him?" She placed a fingernail in her mouth, then immediately dropped it. She'd had a habit of biting her nails in college. "What if he's busy..."

He nodded. He needed to be her friend first, even if the

thought of sending her into another man's arms tore him apart. "Call him. I'll go grocery shopping and we can go look at the fixtures later."

The next thing Winston knew, he was rescheduling the fixture appointment and Gia was preparing to drive to Tennessee. Looking back, he'd known at that moment who she was choosing —Dre.

The record ended and Winston rose to select an album that might fit his mood. He'd found an old record player in the attic, long forgotten by the owners and carted it down to the living room where he'd dusted it off, doubting it still worked.

After going back up to check for stray records and coming up empty, he'd gone to an antique store in town and picked up a few classics to use for testing.

The old player worked after some tweaking and Winston found a new pastime.

Flipping through his growing collection, he stopped and picked up Marvin Gaye's *In the Groove* album.

He cranked the volume up on "Heard it Through the Grapevine" and closed his eyes, feeling the music.

A desperate, rapid knock on the door jolted him awake and he sat up, disoriented for a moment. The record had stopped and the house was quiet.

He stood, stretched, and hurried to the door.

For a moment, he just stood in the doorway staring at the other man. Dre stared right back, as he dared Winston to close the door in his face and Winston's fists balled at his sides. He hated how cock sure Dre was as he stood there in his expensive leather jacket and designer jeans. Dre was one of those men who had the luxury of knowing where he came from and who he was. Winston hadn't known his parents and there were no relatives who claimed him after they died. When he was Dre's age, he still had no clue who he was or what his purpose in life might be.

"Why are you here?" Winston said, his voice tight. Curiosity kept him from slamming the door shut.

"I need your help," Dre said, his voice wavering. The November evening was chilly and the wind whipped around them but Winston didn't invite Dre in.

"You must be desperate if you came to me," Winston scoffed. "What could you possibly need my help with?"

Dre sighed, his shoulders sagging. "I didn't know where else to turn. This is for Gia, not for me. She needs our help."

Winston scowled. "She doesn't want my help." He crossed his arms. "Why would I help you?"

Dre crossed his arms. "Can I come in?"

Winston studied Dre for a moment, unsure of what to say. On the one hand, he didn't want to have anything to do with whatever plan Dre had. If it blew up in Dre's face, Winston wanted to stay far away from it. Gia was already upset with him. No sense in making things worse. On the other hand, Winston could see the desperation and sincerity in Dre's eyes. He sighed, knowing that he couldn't turn Dre away.

"Let me hear what you have to say." Winston stepped aside to let Dre in. "But I'm not doing it for you, Dre. I'm doing it for Gia."

Dre nodded, his shoulders relaxing. He stepped inside and Winston closed the door behind him.

As they made their way to the living room, Winston couldn't help but feel a twinge of jealousy. He had cared deeply for Gia, but it was clear that Dre was the man Gia needed in her life.

Winston motioned at the chair opposite the sofa as he sat. He looked at Dre. "So, what do you need me to do?" he asked.

Dre took a deep breath. "You can run those printers she has, right? Without her, I mean?"

Winston didn't answer immediately, wondering where Dre was going with the questions. He was nervous, Winston could tell, but there was also an undercurrent of excitement coursing through him. "Yeah, I can, but why?"

Dre popped up from his seat. "I need you to modify a

garment, well, technically two. And possibly some stuff for the other guys, depending on how this goes."

They sat down on the couch, and Dre pulled out a tablet from his backpack. "So, here's the thing. I have this silk pajama set and I need your help," Dre said.

Winston nodded, intrigued as he watched Dre pull up a video and play it. "Wow."

Dre grinned. "Yeah. I think this can be done, but I don't know the technical side, which is where you come in."

Winston thought for a moment, weighing the pros and cons. On the one hand, he didn't want to get involved if things didn't work out. But on the other hand, he was genuinely interested in what Dre might do.

Dre spoke up, interrupting his thoughts. "She and her niece were alone at the store during that mess with the protesters. Where were you?"

Dre's tone wasn't exactly accusatory, but Winston took it that way. "Gia told me she didn't need me, so I left." He looked down at the abstract, modern rug on the floor, anything to avoid Dre's hard green eyes boring into him. Judging him.

"Why would she say that? I thought you two were tight?"

He sighed. "She feels like I stirred up trouble by sending Skye to the cabin." He looked back up at Dre's shoulder, unable to meet the man's gaze. "I may have let your real job slip to your mother."

Dre nodded as if a puzzle piece had just fallen into place.

Dre said nothing and Winston continued, needing to justify his actions. "I was hurt... jealous and petty, but it wasn't my place to tell your mother anything. I realize that now."

Shrugging, Dre looked away. "She was going to find out eventually."

He seemed like he had more to say on the subject and Winston waited, but Dre heaved himself back into his chair.

"So, I guess you don't want Gia to know what's going on?

She's in the shop all the time these days which makes it tricky to do this while she's not there."

"Yeah, if I tell her, she'll give me a ton of reasons why it won't work so I want to keep it under wraps for now. How long will it take?"

Winston pursed his lips as he considered the question. "Can I get back to you tomorrow? I actually have a smaller 3D printer here and I want to test some things first. I can do that tonight."

Dre grinned. "Yeah, of course. This is going to be epic if I can pull it all off. And Gia will have all the stores calling."

Studying him closely, Winston asked, "You really think this will help? I'm still getting dirty looks from some of the old ladies around here and I don't see anyone visiting the store."

"I think so. It has to work. You saw the video, right? She put on a brave front but I could tell she was devastated when no one came in the store."

Nodding, Winston cupped his chin with his hand. "Yeah, I saw it." He eyed Dre. "What do you get out of all this?"

"I just want to see her succeed. Gia deserves this." The look on Dre's face hit Winston like a punch to the gut.

"Man, you've got it bad, haven't you?"

Dre winced. "Is it that obvious? Yeah, I'll do anything I can to make her happy. I love her that much." He glanced at Winston. "This shit is awkward. I'm confiding in my competition."

Winston raised his hands in surrender. "Hey, I'm not competition anymore. She wants you."

Shaking his head, Dre exhaled deeply. "She told me she needs time. I'm hoping she chooses me, but it's not looking good."

Despite the circumstances, Winston felt bad for the younger man. "Gia will come around. She's crazy about you from what I can tell."

Dre twisted a black ring on his right thumb. "I hope so. I need to show her I'm committed to us. I was looking at rings while I was in Tennessee, thinking about buying a house here."

Taken aback, Winston stared. "Really? You must be making

good money as a...dancer," he paused. "Or is that your trust fund?"

"The pay is way better than most professional dancers make but I did some cryptocurrency investing a few years ago when it first became a thing and it's done well. And no, I'm not living off my mother's money. I'm making my own way."

Winston considered the man's words. He'd assumed his mother's supermodel earnings supplemented Dre's lifestyle. "Well, if you're serious about buying a house here in Kissing Springs, this house might be an option. The couple who manages the property told me the owners would be willing to entertain an offer," he said. "Gia loves this house. She spent a lot of time here growing up."

Dre nodded, glancing around the living area. "Good to know. I have to win her over first." He looked back at Winston. "You don't want this place? Where are you going to stay?"

Winston ran a hand over his head. "I'm going back to Chicago after the holidays. I think my work here is pretty much done, plus I have a great idea for a startup business. I can help companies implement 3D printing."

"Sounds good." Dre stood up. "Hey, man, I hate that we got off on the wrong foot initially and I appreciate your help with this."

Dre stuck a hand out and Winston, hesitating only a second, took it. "I'll work on this tonight and let you know what I think tomorrow," he said as he walked Dre to the door. "Stop by in the afternoon."

Dre agreed and hurried out into the cold night air.

CHAPTER 14

Gia

During the week of Thanksgiving, Gia sat in her office, going over her finances for what seemed like the hundredth time. This was wasted effort, she knew. Nothing had changed. If she didn't make any sales soon, she'd have to close. There was no more money, no available credit, and no bank would loan her another penny.

She sighed, wanting to bang her head against the table. With Jordyn's help, she'd created some videos and done some lives but that had only resulted in a few online sales. The protesters were still camping out and as long as they did, no one outside her family dared venture into the store.

Gia glanced at the time. She should be putting the "We're Open" sign up in a few minutes but what was the point?

Had she known this would be her fate and all of the long hours, sleepless nights spent worrying and fantasizing about her store were for naught, things might have been different with Dre.

Different how exactly? He was still too young for her.

Her heart said otherwise. Somehow, she'd managed to fall for him, despite fighting like her life depended on it.

This, she knew, was what a messy life looked like up close.

The store's door camera flickered on and Gia saw that

someone was at the door, waving at her. She smiled, reaching for her phone to open the door remotely.

Gia rose and headed to the front.

Her sister-in-law, Noemie, walked in, ready to embrace her. "Hey Sis! The store looks amazing!"

Gia hugged Noemie tightly, relieved to have a friendly face in her store for once. They moved away from the door and Noemie tilted her head toward the protesters milling around outside. "They're still at it, I see."

"Yep. Those old broads are persistent if nothing else." Gia told her about the protesters showing up on opening day and their passive aggressive tactics.

"I'm sorry, Gia. No wonder you look so tired," Noemie said sympathetically.

Gia was tired. Everything in her life lately had been an insurmountable battle up a steep hill. She'd fought and lost the fight to retain her brand from her former partner, then she'd struggled to line up financing for the store and after struggling to get the store open, she was now struggling to keep the doors open.

She shrugged. "Comes with the territory, I guess. Do I look that bad?"

Noemie rubbed her back. "Nothing a bit of concealer and some eyeliner won't fix...but your spark is gone. You usually walk into a room and electrify it. What's really going on? Is it you and Winston? I haven't seen him around lately."

"Well, there's no 'me and Winston' but he's still around. I'm still pissed that he basically sicced Skye on Dre and outed his career to her. I'm trying to be more forgiving and more on but that's easier said than done."

Noemie's mouth dropped. "Is that why Dre quit Derby Nights? Because his mother found out from Winston he was a dancer?"

Shaking her head, Gia motioned to a mini coffee maker on the bar cart by her desk. "We should talk about this over coffee, want a cup?"

Noemie nodded with enthusiasm. "Oh my goodness, yes. Running after Judah is exhausting. School is out this week but I dropped him off at day care so I could get some things done and I've been meaning to come in and check out your shop." She twisted the silver bracelet on her wrist. "And, umm, get something to show off for my anniversary next month."

Gia hid a smile. Her sister-in-law had come from a strict religious upbringing and was still exploring her sensual side. "Of course. We'll create something you love."

Noemie gave her a relieved smile. "Thanks."

She took the steaming cup from Gia and settled into the plush loveseat in front of Gia's desk. "But all that can wait. I want to know more about you and the green-eyed Adonis you've been seeing."

Gia smirked at her sister-in-law's description of Dre. She'd have to pass that along next time she saw him.

"Yeah, so Dre's best friend died in a motorcycle accident and Dre went to his mother's cabin in Tennessee to deal with his grief. I figured he needed a friend and went there to make sure he was ok. It's beautiful there and Skye's cabin is nice, but anyway..." she sipped her coffee, enjoying the warmth. "From what Winston told me, Skye dropped into town unexpectedly to see about the store while I was still at the cabin with Dre and Winston tells her that we're dating like we were up there for a weekend romp and then he tells her that Dre's actually a stripper."

Noemie leaned in. "So, what happened when she got there?"

"Apparently, she told him he needed to leave me alone because he's a distraction and given his profession, not good for my image."

She paused. "And that's when Dre quit Derby Nights?"

As she heard the words aloud, Gia realized how much of a sacrifice Dre had made for her.

"Wow, he quit for you?" Noemie fanned herself. "That's so romantic, but what's he going to do instead? Or is he like a trust fund baby? I know Skye did well during her career."

Gia shook her head. "No, he's determined to make his own way. Skye hasn't supported him since he was in dance school. He wants to start an afterschool performing arts school here in Kissing Springs."

"Oh, that would be amazing! There are so many kids in my school that need a creative outlet." She tilted her head. "That means he's possibly here to stay. How do you feel about that? I know you're itching to go back to New York."

Gia thought about the question for a minute. Initially, her plan had been to get Lush Lingerie up and running and as soon as it took off, she would do a bigger, flagship store in New York. But now, she wasn't so sure moving back to the big city was what she wanted. As much as she complained about her family, she loved them and had gotten used to seeing them regularly.

And while she wouldn't fully admit it to herself, part of her was hoping that Dre would stick around.

"I'm not so sure about New York anymore. I...think my heart may want me to stay here," she said cautiously.

"So...what are you saying? You and Dre? Yes?" Noemie held her mug with both hands, grinning at Gia. "You know Jameson is a big fan. Dre's been teaching dance at the gym. The kids love him...especially the girls." She rolled her eyes.

Her shoulders drooped. "I kept telling myself I didn't want to fall in love, didn't have time for it but it hit me like a bullet train. And I don't know what to do about it." Gia set the coffee cup down and ran a hand over her forehead. "He's so young..."

Noemie sipped her coffee. "What's your concern about his age?"

Gia tapped her lips with her fingertip as she tried to put her thoughts together. "I guess my main concern is that he's going to come to his senses and realize he wants a woman closer to his age so he can have kids. I don't know if I want kids."

"Did you talk to him about this? Does he want kids?" Noemie asked.

Gia sighed. "No, we haven't talked about kids. In my defense, this was supposed to be a one-night thing, not a long term, love you forever kind of situation."

"Sweetie, I'm not judging you, I'm just trying to help you get clarity," Noemie said, shifting in her seat.

Noemie's voice was reassuring and she knew the other woman was trying to help.

"I feel like you're using your guidance counselor skills on me right now." Gia crossed her arms. "And maybe I haven't asked because I don't want to know the answer." She stared down into her cup. "If I'm being totally honest, I'm scared. Scared he'll resent me if we get together and he decides he wants kids in a few years. By then I'll be too old to give him any."

"Speaking from experience, you can have babies after forty. It's no walk in the park, but it can be done. If that's what you want, anyway. But you should talk to him. Is that your only issue with his age?"

Seeing her chance to change the subject, Gia grabbed it. "Speaking of...if you want to bring Judah by while you run errands one day, that'd be fine."

"He'd love hanging out with his aunt and that's very generous of you, but we were peeling back your fears." Noemie's eyes bored into her as the silence in the room grew heavier. Gia's leg jumped. She willed her nerves down.

Maybe she should just say it. Put everything out there. "What if he doesn't love the real me?" she blurted, then covered her mouth with her hand. "I think he loves the confident business woman, not the nerdy awkward girl that I actually am. That girl doesn't attract men like Dre."

Gia stared into her coffee cup, unable to meet her sister-in-law's gaze. "If this store fails, there's no reason for the business woman to stick around."

She left her next words unsaid. And no reason for Dre to stick around either. Tears threatened to fall as Gia sat there, overwhelmed by her admission. She'd never considered this her reason for not exploring serious relationships.

Noemie stood, rushing around the desk to embrace Gia. "Do you know how resilient you are? How talented? I've no doubt you will find a way to make whatever you do a success. And if he doesn't see that, we'll just have Jameson handle him."

They both giggled at that as Gia hugged Noemie back. "Thanks, I didn't realize how much I needed to hear that." This was the sister she'd never had and she was grateful her brother had married her.

After chatting for a few minutes more, Gia led Noemie over to her design lounge where she helped clients visualize how their new lingerie should look. They were both seated in plush chairs facing a fifty-inch LCD screen. As Gia sketched on an e-tablet, Noemie could see the rendering on the monitor.

They were adding the finishing touches to a corset when the front door chimed. Gia's heart raced, hoping it was a new customer.

Then her heart thudded for an entirely different reason.

Dre looked around the store then, seeing them, approached, watching her with those mesmerizing green eyes. She wanted to clutch her pearls and swoon. He looked that good. Dre was wearing a button down light grey shirt and a pair of dark jeans that fit just so in all the right places. Gia imagined ripping the shirt from his chest as his eyes widened in shock. Would he pin her arms above her head and tell her she was a bad girl?

Jeez. What was it about Dre that made her hot as a Kentucky summer? She started to fan herself but caught Noemie smirking at her and dropped her hand.

Love. He loved unabashedly. He'd never wavered in his feelings for her, she realized then.

"Gia, Noemie," he said with a nod.

"Hey Dre, good to see you," Noemie said, giving him a slight finger wave.

Gia smiled, her face heating as he came closer. She could smell his skin and knew he'd just recently showered. He smelled like soap and a woodsy, warm cologne.

He took her hand, sending electric pulses through her. "Do you have a moment? I wanted to talk to you about something."

Noemie jumped up. "It's suddenly warm in here…I could use another cup of coffee. Anyone else want some?"

Shaking her head, Gia kept her eyes on Dre.

"No thanks, I'm good," Dre responded.

"Ok, well, I'll be in the back." She shot Gia a knowing look and winked before walking away.

Dre watched her go then turned back to Gia, his expression questioning. "Are you free tonight after you leave here?"

She nodded, concerned. "Yep, I'll probably start working on whatever Noemie wants. What's up?"

"I don't think I told you I'm back at Derby Nights, helping out with choreographing some new routines for the holiday season."

She shook her head. This was news to her.

"Yeah, it's just for the season though. And I'm not dancing. But I'd like you to come to rehearsal tonight at seven. There's something I want to show you."

Gia's heart raced as she looked up at Dre.

"Sure, I can stop by." She tilted her head, studying him. He seemed happy about something. "Are you going to give me a hint?"

"Nope. You have to come to find out." He leaned down, brushing his lips against hers and heat flooded through her. "See you tonight, beautiful."

Gia felt a flutter in her stomach as she watched him leave. She had always been drawn to him, but she never expected to develop feelings for him. Despite their age difference, he made her feel loved on a level she'd never experienced before.

"Oooo…wait till I tell your brother," Noemie squealed. "What was all that about?"

Startled, Gia whipped around. She'd forgotten Noemie was in the back. "What are you talking about? He wants me to come to his rehearsal tonight," she said, trying to maintain her cool.

"Don't give me that! He was peeling that dress off you with his eyes and you looked like you wanted to lock the door and let him. I know that look."

Was she that obvious? Gia felt her cheeks heating up.

"I might have if you weren't here," she muttered, then in a louder voice asked. "You want to come with me tonight?"

"I heard that. You could have told me to get lost," Noemie said with a laugh. Her dark brown eyes glinted with amusement.

"Tempting, but I have work to do. So, you coming?" Gia asked

Noemie sighed, "I would but Jameson's going to be at the gym late," she said wistfully. "You better call me as soon as you leave. And if he proposes, call me after you say yes."

Gia groaned. "I don't think he's proposing." Though if that kiss was any indication, something told her there would be details to share. Her lips still burned from his brief touch.

"Uh huh, that man wants you, sis. The way he looked at you... like he was on death row and you were a juicy filet mignon." Noemie fanned herself dramatically. "I might have to take Judah to your mother's tonight so I can seduce my husband."

"That's my brother you're talking about, ew," Embarrassed, Gia threw her sketchbook at Noemi who caught it easily. "Now let's get back to this design before I change my mind about letting you live vicariously through me."

Noemie chuckled, her eyes dancing with mirth. "Ok, ok, back to business. But don't say I didn't warn you - that man is going to steal your heart if you're not careful."

Gia smiled, thinking Noemie had no idea how close Dre was to doing just that. Her heart was pretty much gone.

* * *

At seven thirty, Gia walked into the Derby Nights venue where the dancers performed for crowds of screaming women. The space was dark except for spotlights on the empty stage.

Gia recalled the last time she'd come here, ready to confront Dre about his reasons for being in Kissing Springs. That seemed like a lifetime ago, but only six months had passed since then. She spotted Dillon Montgomery, the owner of the venue, sitting in the front and took a seat beside him.

"Hey Dillon, the theater looks amazing," Gia said, looking around.

He grinned. "Thanks, I've got big plans for this place." He turned to look at her. "I've been out of town the last few weeks and missed your store opening but Meadow and I will be there on Black Friday. You know she's been running interference with the anti-technology busybodies but they're stubborn."

She nodded. "Thank you. I appreciate anything she can do."

"Hang in there. We both know the town needs to embrace the change that's happening." He folded his arms. "But I won't get on my soapbox. Dre asked me to sit in on this rehearsal tonight, but he wouldn't tell me why, any ideas?"

"No. He was secretive when he told me to come as well," she said, wondering what he was up to.

Suddenly, the stage lights dimmed, and a piano started to play softly. A muscular male dancer strode onto the stage, wearing a hoodie and boxer shorts. Gia squinted, then tilted her head. That was her design the dancer wore. It looked like the set she'd made for Dre to wear. The set was a dove grey silk that fit the man perfectly. He danced center stage for a minute then an aerial silk dropped onto the stage and a petite woman maneuvered down the silk rope, her body twisting in and out of the material. She wore a shimmery silver body suit.

Once she reached the ground, the man saw her and the trim on the hood of his garment lit up. The woman took his hand and they performed an intricate routine using the silks to spin, twirl, and fly above the stage.

The pair moved to the pace of the piano music, a haunting, sensual slow piece that Gia suspected Dre was playing. It was a beautiful song.

During the course of the routine, the silk set lit up at different points. The dance ended with the woman upside down, her shapely legs wound around the aerial to support her, sharing a kiss with the man as she held him with both arms a few feet off the ground.

Gasping at the beauty of the piece, Gia stood, clapping loudly once the dance was done. She wished she'd recorded the performance so she could watch it again.

Dillon stood as well. "Dre! That was amazing...love the lights!" he called out.

After their performance, the couple stood together, holding hands. At the applause, they bowed slightly and turned toward Dre, who stepped out from backstage. He said something to them then hurried toward Gia and Dillon.

"Thanks, Dillon. You think this is something we can use this season?"

He nodded, pulling out his phone. "Yeah, come by the office tomorrow; we'll work out details. I gotta run, but the crowds will love this!"

Gia watched Dillon hurry off then turned back to Dre who seemed to be holding his breath. "So, what did you think?"

She put a hand to her chest. "That was beautiful! And you used the silk boxer set I sent you? How did you get that to light up?"

"Winston did all of that, I can't take credit, but," he took her hand, "come meet the dancers and you can look at what we came up with."

Gia let him lead her to the stage. Her heart was full as she watched him explain the LED lights that were printed on tulle then the tulle was attached to the hoodie. The combination of Dre understanding the technology she'd been obsessed with over the last few years and showing her what was possible with her creation and of course, Dre being beautiful Dre, had her wanting to pull him backstage to a dark corner and wrap her legs around his waist.

He must have seen where her head was because Dre abruptly thanked the dancers and told the backstage crew he was heading out.

He took her hand again. "Dillon likes the concept so I'm thinking we can use your designs in a few of our numbers this season. That should help with getting the word out. And since they're doing more concerts here, you can be one of the designers on hand."

"Am I correct in assuming that you just made it possible for me to stay in business by partnering with the most successful business here in town?"

He squeezed her hand, grinning at her.

"Am I also correct in thinking you want to stay in Kissing Springs for a while?" She held her breath, waiting on his answer. If he was staying, she had no problem putting her New York plans off until further notice.

"Yes to both. Now, I just have one question for you...are you in or out?"

Gia ran a hand up the row of buttons on his shirt she'd be ripping off once they got back to his apartment. Snaking a hand around his neck, she pulled him toward her for a long, deep kiss. "I'm all in. I love you, Dre."

Epilogue

THE FOLLOWING SPRING

D re glanced out the large conference room window at the beautiful day outside. Maybe once he was done here, he'd have time to run to the wine shop and grab a bottle of champagne. If all went according to plan, there would be cause for a big celebration.

Interrupting his thoughts, Abby Joslin slapped a stack of papers on the conference room table then slid into the seat in front of them.

Frowning at the stack, Dre wondered how much of his life he was signing away and how long the process would take. Looks like that champagne he wanted would have to wait. He glanced over to the closing attorney to find her studying him.

She peered over her reading glasses. "I guess it's a little late now but are you sure she's going to appreciate you buying a house for the two of you without her knowledge, Andreas?"

Dre squirmed under the lawyer's intense gaze. He hoped so. If any of his friends or the guys he worked with asked him for his opinion, he would have vehemently said it was a bad idea. Thanks to his mother and grandmother, he knew the importance of a woman knowing she had a say in a house that she'd be in charge of, but this was a special case.

"I have it on good authority that she's wanted this house since she was a little girl, so yeah, I'm sure," he said with more confidence than he felt. What if Gia didn't want the house? Worse still, what if she didn't want to live with him? That thought sent a jolt of fear through him and he grabbed the glass of water Abby's assistant had provided and gulped it.

Gia was technically still staying at her childhood home with her parents, but she spent most nights at his place. It was small for the two of them, but he found he didn't mind his new domesticated life.

Her parents, initially unable to grasp that Dre, not Winston, was the one coming around for family dinners and gatherings, were warming toward him, helped in part by Jameson's endorsement. He and Jameson got along well, especially since he'd be able to secure tickets to an Alvin Ailey show in New York for him and his wife.

Abby flipped the first document to the signature page and slid it over to him. "I guess we'll find out, won't we?" She summarized what the document said and pointed at the signature line. "Sign here. If all goes well, I want an invite to the housewarming party."

Dre nodded solemnly and signed the papers with an unsteady hand, feeling the weight of his decision to become a first-time homeowner.

As Dre walked out of the conference room, he felt a mixture of excitement and anxiety. He couldn't wait to see Gia's reaction when he showed her the house, but at the same time, he couldn't help but worry that she might not be ready to make such a permanent move. What if she saw this as an act of control? He shook his head, pushing away those thoughts. He knew Gia loved him, and he loved her. If things didn't go the way he planned and she thought moving in together was taking things too fast, he'd give her space to come around.

Before heading to the house, Dre sent a text to Gia's real estate agent, letting him know the plan could proceed as they'd discussed. When his offer for the property had been accepted, Dre had contacted her real estate agent and asked him to bring Gia to the new house under the pretense of it being new to the market.

Driving down the street toward his new home, Dre couldn't help but feel a sense of pride. The neighborhood was older, but the houses were well-kept and the tree lined street was inviting. He could see street parties and neighbor gatherings happening during the warmer months.

He waved at an older woman walking a small dog as he pulled up to the house. The house was perfect. With a picket fence surrounding it, the large yard was ready for cookouts and summer yard games. Dre marveled that he owned a house with a picket fence. He'd assumed that was only done in the movies.

He parked his car in the garage away from view and opened the door to their house. Beyond the porch, the foyer opened into a living room with hardwood floors and a fireplace. Large windows let in plenty of natural light, perfect for curling up and reading a book.

To the right of the living room was a cozy den, ideal as a home office space. And behind that, the spacious kitchen had been updated with granite countertops and stainless-steel appliances. Dre could picture many mornings sharing a pot of coffee with Gia at the kitchen table.

Upstairs were three bedrooms. The master suite took up the right half of the second story. It included a walk-in closet, en suite bathroom with a clawfoot tub and a standing shower. Dre imagined waking up next to Gia in the king-sized bed, sunlight filtering through the bay windows.

The two other bedrooms were nicely sized, one overlooking the backyard garden. The old but sturdy wood floors stretched down the hallway, leading to another full bathroom.

Gia might consider his purchase impulsive and presumptuous, but to Dre it felt right. The place already felt like home to him. He accepted that Gia might not immediately feel the same way, but he was confident she'd come to love the house too.

It had taken a lot of work to get Gia's business off the ground, but now it was thriving. After months of protesting, Gia had finally won over the locals with her collections of custom designed lingerie that flattered every body type and made the wearer feel special.

Dre walked through the living room, admiring the way the sunlight filtered in through the windows, casting a warm glow on the space.

As he leaned against the counter, he heard the sound of a car pulling up outside.

Gia had arrived.

Dre's heart began to race as he heard the sound of footsteps approaching the door. He could hear Gia and her real estate agent chatting excitedly, making their way through the living room towards the kitchen, where he waited, excited to see her reaction.

"I used to play in that yard outside..."Gia stopped when she saw him, her eyes wide.

"Surprise!" Dre said, grinning from ear to ear.

Gia's gaze went from the living room to Dre, her expression one of confusion. "What is this? I thought you were going to Nashville for work?" she asked, taking a step closer to him. "What are you doing here?"

"This is our new home," Dre said, taking her hand. "I bought it for us."

Gia's eyes darted to the real estate agent who was watching them with a knowing smile. "You bought a whole house?" she asked, a smile slowly spreading across her face. "How did you know this was the house I wanted?"

He shrugged. "Winston convinced the owners to sell before he left. He told me about the girls who lived here when you were growing up and how you loved coming to this house to play with them."

Gia's eyes widened in surprise. "I can't believe you did this," she said, her voice filled with emotion. "It's beautiful."

"I know this is a big step and I realized you might not be ready but," Dre pulled her close, wrapping his arms around her waist as they stood in the kitchen. "I wanted to give you something special," he said, leaning in to kiss her.

She grinned at him. "Are you kidding? When can we start moving in? I love my parents but I miss having my own space. And this house is perfect, oh my goodness I can't believe you bought us a house..." she murmured again.

Gia's lips met his, and the two of them shared a deep, passionate kiss. As they pulled away, Dre looked into her eyes, seeing a swirl of emotions.

"I love you," he said softly.

"I love you too," Gia replied, leaning in for another kiss.

The real estate agent cleared his throat from behind them causing them to break apart. "Well, it looks like my work here is done," he said with a smile. "I'll leave you two to enjoy your new home."

Dre and Gia watched as the agent made his way out of the house, leaving them alone in the kitchen.

He turned to her, an eyebrow raised, ready to ask if she'd be interested in christening the house right away when Gia spoke. "We should check out the bedroom, shouldn't we? And make sure the walls are sturdy enough to support me?"

He loved that they were on the same page. He was about to scoop her up and press her against the first wall he could find when there was a knock at the door.

"It's my family, isn't it? With perfect timing as usual." Gia glanced out the front window.

"Probably. I told Jameson I was closing today." And he might have asked him to bring the rest of Gia's family over, just in case she wasn't on board with the house idea, figuring she wouldn't attempt to strangle him with her family watching.

Dre opened it to find Gia's family crowded against each other, grinning like they had all just purchased a new house.

Jameson elbowed his way in and Dre stepped back as the rest of the family filed into the house.

"Congratulations, you two!" said Jameson, walking in holding his son Judah with Noemie and daughter Jordyn following close behind. "Once you get settled, time to think about a wedding, right, Dre?"

Gia's mother and father stepped in taking in the empty house.

Once again, the Mitchells wasted no time getting right to the point. They'd talked about marriage, but Dre knew Gia wasn't quite ready for that leap. "Maybe, but that's not my call," he glanced at Gia, who rolled her eyes behind her brother's back.

"We're doing things at our own pace." Gia folded her arms. "This is a big enough step for me right now. And we've got a lot going on with the store and getting Dre's performing arts school off the ground."

Gia's mother, Carla, spoke up. "You know if I suggest anything, Gia does the exact opposite, so I think you should wait a few years before you get married, sweetheart." She winked at Dre.

"Really, Ma?" Gia sighed. "Can we just enjoy this moment before you start planning our wedding?" She motioned to the champagne bottle in Noemie's hand. "Is that for us? Let's pop that bottle and drink to new beginnings."

"You don't have to tell me twice," she dug into the baby bag on her hip and pulled out a set of plastic flutes. "Dre, you want to do the honors since this is your house?"

"I'm just saying, Gia, you aren't getting any younger. If you're going to have babies..."

"You know what, I'd love a glass of champagne, thanks!" Gia said brightly.

Dre nodded, taking the bottle from Noemie and removing the foil. He couldn't help the grin on his face. Gia's family was warm, opinionated, and loved to hang out with each other. He didn't mind the wedding and family talk. At least it wasn't coming from him.

As he poured the bubbly drink into each glass, Gia handed them out.

Jonah reached for his mother's glass. "No alcohol for you yet, sweet pea. This is for Mommy." Noemie held the glass out of his reach.

"A toast to Gia and Dre!" Jameson raised his glass. "As is the Mitchell way, we have another set of successful businesses to celebrate! Cheers!"

Everyone tapped the plastic glasses together and sipped. Jameson downed his and took Judah from Noemie. "Speaking of Mitchell businesses, we're all going to Cousin Saxon's Book Fair next week, right? I told him we would come."

There were nods of agreement as Dre frowned. "Who's Cousin Saxon?"

Gia's dad spoke up. "That's my brother's son. He's around Jameson's age and started a bookstore over near the highway, closer to the distilleries. It's called The Book Barrel cause he sells bourbon too. Yeah, we'll be there but then we're headed to Puerto Vallarta."

Smacking her lips, Jordyn piped up. "Gramma! When are we doing a family trip? I wanna lay in the sun too!"

Judah clapped his hands like he agreed.

Carla Michell swirled the flute in her hand. "That trip is for our anniversary, but Jordyn, you seem to be the event planner in the family. Gia's grand opening for Lush was well run, why don't you put together something. Maybe we can go on a cruise for your graduation next summer?" She then turned toward Dre and he could see the wheels turning in the older woman's head. "That would make a nice wedding venue, a cruise, don't you think?"

Gia ran a hand over her face. "Ok, look, I love y'all but if you keep it up, Dre is going to put us all out. Let's let the man enjoy his new space in peace."

As the family filed out, Dre wrapped his arms around her. "You're staying, right?"

"Yep, we've got unfinished business."

When he looked into Gia's eyes, he knew their home would be filled with love, laughter, and memories that they would cherish for the rest of their lives.

* * *

The End

Thank you for reading Gia's story! If you want to read about how Gia and Dre first met, check out the story One Hot Night in Nashville in the Ms. CEO anthology.

The office isn't the only place they like to be on top...
The heroines in this anthology are feisty, sassy, and know what they want in and outside the boardroom. They fought their way to raise their empire from the ground up

and won't take no crap from anyone. Time is money, and they have none to waste. Our women fight to stay at the top...

* * *

And check out the next story about the Kissing Springs Mitchells.

Grumpy bookstore owner Saxon Mitchell isn't looking for love but he can't seem to avoid his ex-wife's publicist Love Whitfield and eventually decides maybe he doesn't want to. But his ex-wife has other plans.

* * *

If this is your first Welcome To Kissing Springs novel, check out Gia's brother Jameson's story in Silver Santa.

Happily divorced high school guidance counselor Noemie Saint has moved back to Kissing Springs to be closer to her mother after her father's death. She wouldn't say she's avoiding the ex that broke her heart twenty years ago, but she's certainly not going out of her way to run into him.

Twenty years ago, he chose to do the right thing and let Noemie go. Now that she's moved back to town and they are both single, he's sure he can convince her they belong together.

She wants one night, he wants forever. Can this second chance couple make some Christmas magic?

Welcome to Kissing Springs

MULTI-AUTHOR STEAMY ROMANCE SERIES

Welcome to Kissing Springs, Kentucky!

In this new collection of steamy romance, nine authors bring you standalone stories from single dads to second chances, ex-military to sports romances all set in the small town of Kissing Springs, Kentucky.

Read all 27 books across 3 seasons by 9 authors.

Santa Season:

https://www.kissingsprings.com/santa-books

Sunshine Season:

https://www.kissingsprings.com/sunshine

Bourbon Season:

https://www.kissingsprings.com/bourbon

Follow Us To Kissing Springs

Join us in our Facebook group, celebrating all things about the small town of Kissing Springs, the romance capital of the South.

We share recipes, cocktails, tips, freebies, cover reveals, author insights, and more fun.

Go to: Welcome to Kissing Springs Reader Group on Facebook.

facebook.com/groups/1601547460211768

Sign up for monthly news and updates:

www.kissingsprings.com/welcome